MORGANA MAGE

IN THE
ROBOTIC AGE

Amy Bond

2 PALMER STREET,
FROME, SOMERSET
BA11 1DS

Text © Amy Bond 2021
Illustration © Nan Lawson 2021

First published in Great Britain in 2021
Chicken House
2 Palmer Street
Frome, Somerset BA11 1DS
United Kingdom
www.chickenhousebooks.com

Cover and interior design by Steve Wells
Cover illustration by Nan Lawson
Typeset by Dorchester Typesetting Group Ltd
Printed and bound in Great Britain by CPI Group (UK) Ltd, Croydon CR0 4YY

The paper used in this Chicken House book is made from
wood grown in sustainable forests.

1 3 5 7 9 10 8 6 4 2

British Library Cataloguing in Publication data available.

PB ISBN 978-1-912626-52-6
eISBN 978-1-913322-27-4

A MESSAGE FROM CHICKEN HOUSE

I love all the technology I have in my house – but what if it stops advising me what to do and starts ordering me around? After all, I am pretty lazy sometimes, and not very efficient! If things go *really* wrong, I might need an engineer . . . or maybe some magic help . . . Perhaps the answer is a bit of both – imagination and robots working together! Amy Bond shows how spells and robots collide and ultimately save the day. Fantastic, fast and full of unexpected friendships, this first novel about magic and machines is fizzing with fun!

BARRY CUNNINGHAM
Publisher
Chicken House

For Mam and Dad

Chapter One

Morgana often wished that she wasn't a witch, but at times like this she simply longed to be a better one. It wasn't that she particularly wanted to fly, but she did hate being laughed at, and she could hear the sniggers breaking out around her. Well, just above her, really, as all the other kids were floating in the air on the various objects they had managed to levitate. Morgana remained stubbornly earthbound. She had picked a clichéd old broomstick on which to try getting afloat, thinking it might be nice and light.

'Come on, you stupid broom,' she muttered, eyes screwed shut.

In desperation she tried a little leap into the air to get things started, but only managed to trip over her own feet and fall on her face.

Everyone was roaring with laughter now. Unable to concentrate on their spells because they were cackling so hard, most of the other kids came crashing back to earth. Only her best friend Esther was composed enough to stay airborne in her old tin bath.

Morgana's mum looked helplessly at the pile of a dozen or so children she was supposed to be teaching, and let out a sigh.

'OK, everyone, I think we can leave it there for the morning. But we have some hard work to do after lunch. This afternoon we'll move on from levitation to flight – we'll try and really take off.' She shot Morgana a look that was half pity, half exasperation. They both knew she had no chance of succeeding at that exercise.

Esther glided down to her side. Morgana could tell she was going to try and say something comforting.

'Don't bother,' said Morgana. 'I'm just hopeless.'

Before Esther had a chance to disagree, Mr Roche appeared behind her. 'Still no improvement, I see,' he said. He cast a withering gaze over Morgana, the raven perched on his shoulder directing an even more searching stare over her.

'Well, at least she's attending class,' said Ms Garcia. She didn't look at Morgana, though her stoat peered at her from a pocket in her cloak. 'Even if there is still no evidence of any magical ability.'

'Mum!' said Esther. 'That's not fair!'

Morgana knew she shouldn't storm away from the village elders, but if they were going to discuss her as if she wasn't there, she might as well leave them to it. And as rude as she might seem, she knew she could get a lot ruder if she stuck around.

She stomped past the vegetable patch and frightened some of the sheep as she marched by the paddocks. She was still furious as she reached the village, if you can call fifteen rickety cabins a village. She burst into the family cabin with such force she almost knocked over the broom that was sweeping the floor by itself, and sat in a huff at the table.

She didn't even look up when her mum entered the cabin a few minutes later and took a seat beside her. 'You could apply yourself more, Morgana,' she said, as Morgana's wooden bowl, loaded with lunchtime stew, floated in from the campfire outside and plopped gently in front of her. 'If you had been here for the last lesson . . .'

'It wouldn't have made a difference, Mum. The magic in me just isn't strong enough.'

'Magic doesn't come from within you,' said her mother, her voice stern now. 'You know that much at least, Morgana. The magic is in the world around you – in the air, in the light, in the water, in the fire. You could connect yourself to the elements as strongly as anyone else if you would open yourself up to them, try to understand them. You will have a natural link to one of the elements and that will open the door to the others – you just need to figure out which one is special to you. And you need to practise.'

'I'm already trying my best,' Morgana mumbled.

She stuck her spoon in the stew and stirred it glumly. 'Everyone's so mean about my magic, though. Either judging me or laughing at me. It's not very motivational.'

'See, this is why I'm trying to help you,' said Morgana's older brother Turlough, who had just arrived, wrestling with a squirrel he was trying to persuade to sit in the hood of his cloak. 'You should take advantage of having a brother who's in line to be a village elder.'

Elders of the community were any witches or warlocks who had familiars. Animals chose magic folk as companions very rarely, but Turlough convinced himself every other week that some creature had taken a shine to him. This squirrel was the latest, now getting tangled in his brown curls as he tried to escape. Morgana was impressed that her brother managed to continue:

'I'll help you improve your magic. Everyone will treat you better when they see you're just like the rest of us.'

But what if I'm not *like the rest of you?* thought Morgana. She knew her brother wanted to protect her, help her be happy. But the only way he saw of doing this was making her like everyone else. Even her own brother couldn't accept her as she was.

Her father came in from feeding the animals.

'I'm going to have to head down to the city for some potion supplies this afternoon,' he said. 'I was thinking perhaps Morgana could come down with me?'

Morgana raised her head from the table eagerly, but tried to keep her face as composed as possible. She knew it wasn't something she should be excited about: if anything, a trip to the city would generally be considered a punishment, as it meant having to spend time surrounded by the city folk who hated them, and their unnatural machines. But the city had always fascinated Morgana. She knew it shouldn't, but it did. She had already been planning to try to disappear into the forest to avoid the humiliation of the afternoon's magic lesson. She had a favourite tree that gave her the best view of the city below. She could spend hours gazing down, imagining a life where it didn't matter that no spells worked for her. She could hardly believe that she was going to get to visit it for real – if her mum would agree, that is.

'Well . . . isn't she a bit young?' Morgana's mother glanced at her doubtfully. Morgana had to clamp her mouth shut to stop herself protesting. She was eleven, and Turlough had visited the city when he was ten. 'And there are flying lessons this afternoon . . .'

Morgana's dad shrugged. 'She'll have to go there eventually,' he said. 'Needs to know what we're up against. Besides, it's not like she'll be going on her own. I'll be with her the whole time.'

Mum pursed her lips, sighed and nodded her agreement.

Chapter Two

'I heard it was a tough lesson this morning,' her father said as they traipsed down the mountainside. 'Don't worry, Morgana. Your magic will manifest in its own time, in its own way.'

Morgana didn't respond. She barely even heard him. She was too enthralled by the sight before them.

The city rose in challenge to the mountains, its metal and glass shining brightly in the clear morning sunlight. Three great discs supported its buildings, the tallest of the skyscrapers reaching higher than the mountains. But the greatest of its buildings was a tower encircled by all three layers, stretching right the way up the centre till it pierced the clouds.

Morgana stayed close by her father's side as they walked down the road to the city, watching as road cars streamed up the highways, circled by the designated airstreams that the air cars flew through. Morgana wondered how these didn't collide with the trains that criss-crossed the roads so quickly you could barely see them, sometimes disappearing underground in a blur, sometimes heading up vertical rails to the highest heights of the city.

On the tops of the buildings, sudden bursts of light broke out intermittently. She pointed up at them. 'What are those lights, Dad?'

'People arriving by teleportation,' he said, the disapproval clear in his voice. 'They have some means of disappearing from one place and appearing in another.'

Morgana watched the flashes of light, mesmerized. *No need for flying,* she thought.

'Come on,' her father said, tugging her along. 'We've not got long before the shops close.'

Morgana knew it wasn't right to be so entranced by a city full of people that hated witches and warlocks, people who had tried to ban her community's way of life, but she couldn't help letting out a disappointed sigh. She knew any shops her father would be visiting would be in the lower quarters of the city, where some magic folk still lived, though magic itself was outlawed. This was not the side of the city that she hung from the trees trying to catch a glimpse of.

They were getting closer to the city now, and she could see they were heading for the bottom of the three great discs. She held her breath as they reached their destination, stepping nervously on to the great slab of the metropolis. She felt afraid that she might be the one who would tip the balance and send the whole thing crashing down.

As they made their way further into the city, the streets became busier. Morgana couldn't stand it at first, she felt she might suffocate in the crowds. She never could have imagined as many people existed in the whole world as she could see walking down the one street they were on. All these people seemed completely mad too, chatting away freely with the air.

'Who was he talking to, Dad?' Morgana asked, as they passed a middle-aged man having a very serious conversation with no one she could see.

Her dad replied in a grim voice, 'They have earbuds, Morgana – tiny machines that let them speak to people far away, as if they're right in front of them. It's unnatural.'

Morgana's eyes widened. It sounded rather wonderful to her, not having to try to send messages on the wind.

Every so often strange-looking figures would appear that looked like they were made from a silvery metal, similar to the pots and pans at home. 'What are they?' she asked her father, tugging at his sleeve again.

'Robots,' he hissed, eyes narrowed above his bushy beard. 'Stay well away from them. They are the most dangerous creatures.'

Morgana eyed the next robot she saw more

suspiciously, but as she watched it approaching, she stumbled over a silver boot. When she lifted her gaze she saw that it led to the leg of a jumpsuit that at first appeared to be silver, but became iridescent and woven through with every imaginable colour when the light hit it. A head piled high with blonde hair and a nose scrunched up in distaste topped off the ensemble.

'Ugh,' said the woman to no one Morgana could see. 'I almost fell over a little witch child. Why do they even let them in the city? They should be kept down in the Undercity.'

Morgana wasn't surprised by the rudeness of the woman. The only city folk she had encountered before were the education inspectors, a load of brutes who burst into the woods every so often. Supposedly they were searching for school-age children. In reality, it was just an excuse to mess up the camp and threaten the magical population. No city folk actually wanted witch and warlock children in their schools.

The woman strutted away, elbowing Morgana's father as she went. The robot that Morgana had been trying to avoid followed close behind the woman, carrying a number of brightly coloured shopping bags and boxes. Morgana suppressed a tingling desire to reach out and touch the creature as it passed.

There seemed to be robots everywhere, some trailing behind people like the one they had just encountered, some just strolling purposefully through the streets themselves, and others that were hard at work. She saw one cleaning windows, another directing traffic.

'Don't worry,' her father said in a reassuring voice as she twisted her head around, trying to take in everything around her. 'We'll be away from this sort of crowd soon enough. There are some of our own kind in the Undercity still, and that's where we're heading.'

Morgana tried to hide her disappointment as they left the wide thoroughfare they were on and began to climb down a long flight of stairs to the ground level of the city, below the first of the floating discs.

The buildings here were low – mostly four or

five storeys high – and built from a dull red brick that was a stark contrast to the brilliant white, reflective glass and pale pastels of the towers above. They were also more precarious-looking. Most seemed to be leaning on each other to stay upright, walls sloping and bricks crumbling away in parts. Though there were fewer people around, the narrow winding cobbled lanes felt just as crowded as the streets above.

Morgana's father paused outside what seemed to be a shop, though there was no indication of what it might be selling. 'I'm just going to pop in here for some supplies. Best you wait outside. I'll just be a moment.'

As soon as her father passed over the threshold Morgana began to get nervous. She felt very small and insignificant, and thought she might get trampled underfoot by all the people pushing past without so much as a glance at her. But soon she was wishing she had remained unnoticed.

'And who might you be, little one?' came a whisper in her ear.

Morgana jumped so violently that she

wondered if her skeleton had left her body. She turned to see the crinkled face of a wizened old woman peering at her, so hunched over that she was at eye level. She was dressed in a similar style of cloak to the ones they wore in the mountains, but hers was so encrusted with dirt and grime it seemed to be dragging her down. She smiled a twisted smile at Morgana, who heard all her mother's warnings echoing in her head.

There are some strange characters in the city, she had told her as they'd prepared to leave. *Even the witches and warlocks below are extremely suspicious of new faces. Be very careful.*

So she didn't respond to the woman's question, but backed away from her, only to bump into a man she hadn't noticed, standing right behind her. He too was incredibly aged, with yellow skin hanging in folds about his face. Morgana could just see a few brown teeth in his mouth as he began to talk to her.

'No need to be rude, young lady. Why don't you just answer the question? What's your business here?'

Morgana's mouth was so dry she couldn't have spoken if she'd wanted to. She could feel her chest quivering with the racing of her heart, and couldn't think what to do other than get away from them as quickly as she could, but as she tried to slip away the old man grabbed her shoulder, his bony fingers holding her tight.

'No need to be running off now, when we're just trying to have a friendly chat,' he said in a voice that sounded anything but friendly.

Suddenly another figure moved into the space through which she had been planning to make her break for freedom. The newcomer was a younger man, short and stocky, with a thick neck.

'Stranger, is it?' he asked gruffly. 'Could be a little robot spy?'

'Aargh,' said the old man, spitting on the ground. 'You know as well as I that they can't make them look like people. They have their laws too. She could still be a spy, all the same.'

'What's to be done with her?'

Morgana didn't give them a chance to decide. She yanked herself free from the old man's clutches and aimed a solid kick at the younger man's shins. He let out a howl, and she took off like a greyhound between their legs. Not until she was at the end of the street did she risk a quick glance over her shoulder. She saw that she was being pursued – not only by the original trio that had cornered her, but a number of stragglers who had joined to give chase.

But Morgana was faster and smaller. She darted through the tightly packed streets, quickly leaving the angry group lagging behind, and dashed into an alleyway, glancing around for someplace to hide. A mangy cat hissed at her from behind an overflowing bin. She held her breath and leapt behind the rubbish heap, crouching to the ground.

As she peered out anxiously for the people chasing her, she started to feel frightened. In trying to lose them, she'd taken a few sharp turns and now didn't know where she was. Even if she could remember how to get back to her father, how would she get past those horrible city witches and warlocks?

The cat who'd hissed at her before now

approached her timidly, risking a couple of gentle head nudges. Morgana patted it gently on the back, then snatched her hand away at the sharp coldness she felt. She inspected the animal more closely and saw areas of metal between the islands of filthy ginger fur that partially covered it. At her first touch it had lost all fear and was now coiling around her legs, purring madly, gazing up at her with glowing green eyes. Morgana's fear melted away as she looked down at its cute little face.

'Good kitty,' she said, giving it a more enthusiastic stroke, now rather enjoying the sensation of fur passing over sleek metal.

This moment of peace didn't last long, as a whirring sound was travelling down the alleyway. It seemed to be making straight for them. As Morgana looked up, a silver figure stopped suddenly in front of where she was hiding and pushed the bin aside. She looked up, mouth open.

It was a robot!

Its metal body was shining brightly against the dingy alley. It was shaped like a man on top but, unlike the first robot she had encountered, this was where its human similarities ended. Below the waist was a single column leading to a pair of wheels.

'I am a robot of the city police force,' it said in a clear and steady voice, which Morgana found comforting in its lack of emotion. 'Please see my official identification,' it continued, producing a badge from a compartment in its torso. 'I sense that you are a minor in distress. Can I be of assistance?'

Morgana stood silent and baffled for a moment, but the creature showed no sign of impatience.

'I'm lost,' she said eventually in a small voice.

'Were you accompanied by a parent?'

'Yes, my father.'

'Would he still be in a radius of one kilometre based on where you left him and average human walking speed?'

'I think so,' answered Morgana, not quite sure she understood the question.

'I will determine his whereabouts,' said the robot. A strange antenna appeared from his head, touched Morgana gently on the forehead, and then circled around in the air. It let out a ping, pointing in what Morgana guessed to be the direction she had come from.

'I have identified a grown male sharing your DNA in this direction. Will you permit me to escort you to him? If you would prefer, another officer can be called to bring him here while I wait with you.'

'I'll go with you,' said Morgana, without hesitation. She knew this thing wasn't a real person, but it had shown her more kindness and consideration than any human she had encountered today. She reached up to take the metal hand it offered her.

In this fashion they made their way back through the streets, the creature she now thought of as Kitty also strutting by their side. There was no need to worry about the crowds now, as everyone disappeared from their path, though Morgana noticed some evil looks shot their way. Eventually she spotted her father, circled by the same crowd that had chased her away, but she didn't fear them with this metal policeman by her side.

'Dad,' she cried, waving her free hand.

'Morgana!' her father replied, rushing forward to snatch her from the robot, without even acknowledging him. Morgana tried to turn in her father's arms to give her own farewell to the police robot, but he was already shooting off down the road, leaving a mutinous-looking mob in his wake. Kitty pressed close to Morgana's leg.

'Just an innocent little witch, you say,' said the stooped old woman to Morgana's dad. 'Yet she wouldn't say a word to us, and then comes cavorting back with that robot scum. Spies, the pair of you, I reckon.'

'Come on, Morgana,' said her dad, shooting the woman an angry stare. 'Time to go home, I think.'

As she walked away, Morgana glanced down to see whether Kitty was following, only to find the creature gone. She turned around. One of the witches seemed to be preparing to kick the little cat into the gutter. That decided Morgana on the spot: Kitty was coming home with them. She dashed back and grabbed at the cat, a boot meant for its side catching her in the hand instead.

'I've got you, Kitty,' she murmured to the robot,

hurrying after her father to the stairs before he'd even realized she was gone.

He didn't stop until they were back on the first level.

'Are you all right?' he asked Morgana quietly, then without waiting for an answer, pulled her into a hug. She was still holding her feline machine tightly in her arms. 'What's this?' Dad said, noticing Kitty. 'Morgana, you can't bring that thing home. Your mother will kill me.'

'She won't know! I promise I'll keep her hidden. Please, Dad?' Morgana looked up at him with the big eyes she knew he found it impossible to resist.

'Well, all right,' he sighed at last. 'But mind you keep it a secret. If your mother and brother see it, I'll never hear the end of it.'

They started walking together, back out towards the mountains. 'Those people were scary,' Morgana said.

'They have to put up with a lot, city witches and warlocks,' he said. 'Makes them very mistrustful. But so would you be if you had to deal with the rest of these city folks every day. Trying to drive you out, forbidding you from practising magic within the city, and sending down spies to try and catch you in the act. When we came out of the shadows it was because we thought that non-magic people were enlightened enough to accept our magic, but although they laugh at us, deep down they still fear our powers. They don't like to admit it, though – that's why they have to adopt more subtle forms of persecution.'

'Like the education inspections?' Morgana asked.

Morgana's dad nodded. 'We've got it easy, though. I think the witches and warlocks who still live in the city would be better off in the mountains, but I understand that they don't want to leave their homes. It would be like giving in.'

Morgana gave him a look that made it clear that he wasn't going to instil any sympathy in her right now, not after what she had just been through.

'Well, anyway, I think we had better be getting home. I think you've had enough adventure for a lifetime today. I can't imagine you'll ever want to come back to the city again.'

Morgana didn't answer. She wasn't listening. She was already planning her next visit – not to the Undercity, but to the city itself, with its crazy clothes and amazing technology . . . and best of all, the robots. But if she was going back, she was going to need some help.

Chapter Three

Esther wouldn't be persuaded at first. No matter how rhapsodically Morgana described the wonders waiting for them at the foothills of the mountains the day after her visit, the city held no interest for Esther. They were in the shed-like den they'd built together, down by the river, where Esther kept all manner of her magical works in progress and Morgana kept a map of the city that she'd found among her parents' old papers. Judging by its yellowing paper, she thought it dated from the earliest days of the city's existence, showing its three layers in such intricate detail that it took up almost the full height of the wall. She would pore over it for hours.

'Who needs the city? There are enough incredible things for me to discover right here,' Esther said as she examined a piece of bark with a magnifying glass. 'These woods would still be revealing mysteries to me if I were to study them for centuries.'

Morgana rolled her eyes. If Esther wasn't to be persuaded by words, she would have to be shown how cool the city could be. It was time for Morgana's *pièce de résistance*. 'But nothing so amazing as *this*!' she cried, lifting Kitty from her satchel and plonking her down on the table at the centre of the den.

Esther raised an eyebrow. 'Well, it seems a pretty crude piece of work to me,' she said dismissively.

'How dare you,' said Morgana, covering Kitty's ears. Morgana was already very protective of her new companion. She was starting to see the appeal of having a familiar.

Poor Kitty was already having a hard time,

cooped up in Morgana's bedroom. Morgana had promised her father she would keep her hidden away, but she could already tell it wasn't going to be easy. The cat might have been mechanical, but she was still incredibly curious.

'Well, I'm going again anyway,' proclaimed Morgana. 'Kitty needs to get out. If you want to let me go alone, on your conscience be it!'

As usual, guilt did the trick.

'Oh, all right,' said Esther, putting down her magnifying glass. 'If you insist on going down to that place then I really should keep an eye on you. When do you want to go?'

Over the next months, they sneaked away as often as Esther would let them risk it. At first, they simply wandered around, Morgana gazing at the robots and the towers and soaking up the atmosphere. Then they found the junkyard, a treasure trove of cast-off mechanical pieces which Morgana spent hours searching through. Slowly, Esther's cauldron, and phials and herb samples were pushed aside to make space for the bits of machinery and scrap metal that Morgana had scavenged.

'You don't even know what any of this is,' Esther grumbled as they hauled one load up the mountainside.

'I'm getting to know it,' said Morgana.

And as Esther studied her plants, and worked on her spells, Morgana pored over the bits of metal that now littered their den. She had even found some old machine diagrams among the rubbish and tried making things herself from the scraps, Esther providing the fire power needed to shape the metal.

Sometimes, as Morgana strolled through the woods now, or attended her catastrophic magic lessons, the trees around her almost melted away, and she was on layer number two, making her way from the town hall to the middle section of the RoboCorp tower.

Deep down she knew that the world she was living in was an illusion, and it couldn't last for ever . . .

Turlough burst in on the den one day, a few months after Morgana's first trip to the city. She froze, holding part of a reconstructed robot arm, her cheeks suddenly burning.

'I know, I know, this place is private. But I was just passing . . . and—' He stopped abruptly as his brain made sense of what he was looking at. His mane of curls shook gently as he trembled with rage. His mouth hung open in shock, contorting in fury as he tried to spit out his words. 'What's *this*?'

Morgana set down the arm, determined to stay calm although it felt like the happiness she'd been building up for months was crashing around her.

'This is my collection,' she said quietly.

'Collection? Collection? Collection of what?!' Turlough looked horrified.

'It's just some stuff,' Esther said, stepping forward to stand at Morgana's side. 'It's not a big deal.'

'Not a big deal?!' he yelled. 'It's obvious that Morgana has turned her back on our community completely! These machines go against the natural order at the heart of our magic. And they are made by people who would destroy our way of life.'

'I'm not turning my back on the community. I'm just following my own interests for once. And it's not like anyone wants me to be a part of the community anyway. Everyone has already made it clear that I'm a useless witch.'

'But I've offered to help you,' Turlough said, the anger in his voice replaced with hurt. 'We could have worked on your magic, but you never even tried. Instead you surround yourself with the works of a society that hates us.'

'They don't even know us,' said Morgana. 'Maybe if we weren't so closed off and mistrustful—'

Esther felt the need to interrupt here. 'Morgana, don't kid yourself. It's not *our* fault that they don't know us. You know they have no interest in understanding witches and warlocks.'

'Yes,' agreed Turlough. 'They're quite happy to remain ignorant of our powers – and scared and jealous.'

'Maybe they were jealous of magic once,' said Morgana, warming to her subject. 'But they've got powers of their own now. They haven't been sitting in the dark for centuries brooding over us, like we have over them. They've created light and flight for themselves, and so much else! And meanwhile, we're happy to remain ignorant of the wonders they've achieved. Probably afraid that we might have to admit they've surpassed us.'

Esther looked shocked at this speech. She was standing at Turlough's side now, Morgana noticed.

'Morgana, you know as well as I do that they needed our powers to save their precious city at the end of the last war. We revealed ourselves to help them, and they turned on us, banned our magic from a city that was only standing because of it,' Esther said angrily. 'And you're taking *their* side?'

Morgana couldn't believe Esther had turned against her – she'd thought her best friend had understood! She was speechless with anger.

The three children glared at one another for a few seconds. Perhaps to break the awkward silence, Kitty let out an ill-advised meow. Turlough glanced down at her, his lip curling. But Morgana thought he looked a bit frightened of her as well.

'What's that . . . thing?!'

'Don't take it out on Kitty just because you don't have a familiar.'

'HA!' said Turlough, trying to look amused, though Morgana could tell she had upset her brother. 'As if that thing counts as a familiar. You clearly have no understanding of magic, so don't worry, Morgana. I won't try to help you any more.' He opened the door of the den.

Kitty leapt at the opportunity to escape and bounded towards him eagerly, but let out a startled yelp as the door slammed shut. Morgana ran over – the poor creature's paw had got caught in the door, and was bent almost completely out of shape.

'Oh no,' said Morgana. 'Poor Kitty. . . I need to get her a new paw. I can't leave her like this.' She looked up at Esther. 'Look, I'm sorry about the argument, I didn't mean to upset you. Please can we go to the city?'

'OK,' said Esther, her frown softening slightly as she watched Kitty struggle. 'But this is the last time I'm going with you. I don't want to be a part of it any more.'

'All right,' said Morgana. She was starting to

understand the trouble this whole thing might cause, and she didn't want to get Esther involved more than she already was. 'I won't ask you ever again.'

Chapter Four

The two girls stood at the base of the city's huge central tower, RoboCorp headquarters. Morgana could feel her giddiness escalate as they carefully approached this great monolith of industry.

They were standing on the lowest disc, the manufacturing level of the building, though they weren't heading for the gate where the workers were streaming in and out for their shifts. Morgana didn't understand how they could look so miserable when they were on their way to help create such incredible machines. She would have loved to join them, and see the wonders within, but as usual they were heading for the scrap yard at the other side.

'It's just a big mess of metal,' Esther said, sighing as they reached the fence. During previous excursions, Morgana had contented herself with staying outside the boundary, collecting stray materials from the perimeter. But this time, they'd have to go through. Kitty's new foot was too specific to chance upon.

Esther stretched out her hands, sparks flying from them as she tried to force the bars apart by magic, her frown deepening in concentration. 'This is hard, you know. Magic doesn't work on metal. I have to use the air to try and warp them. I'm not sure I can gather enough strength for it.'

'Keep trying,' urged Morgana, reaching out to touch the bars. A bright yellow spark of magic flew from her fingers and she snatched her hand away. Weird. She didn't generally have enough power to spark at will, let alone randomly.

She stared at the bars her friend was trying to

part, willing Esther to succeed. She knew the fence was steel, and not pliable at all, but they *had* to bend, just a little, or else Kitty wouldn't be able to walk.

She was so caught up in her wishing that it took her a while to notice the bars had warped slightly, just enough to let them slip through. Morgana rushed in past Esther, who was frowning as she looked between her hands and the fence.

'Strange . . .' she said.

Morgana didn't wait to find out what was strange. She was already blissfully diving through a heap of steel and tin. 'Oh, this could do for a leg,' she said, plucking out a copper cylinder. 'But I can't see anything that would work as a paw.' She stowed the cylinder away in her satchel anyway.

'What about this?' asked Esther, holding up a lump of metal.

Morgana moved over to her to inspect it more closely. 'The size is pretty much right, but it's too solid and heavy. Kitty would have a hard time dragging that around.'

She turned back towards the pile she was looking through, when there was a screeching noise from the factory doors. Esther clutched at her sleeve.

'Come and help me in the scrap yard, Igor,' yelled a voice just out of sight. 'We need to check the work the collection robots have been doing.'

Esther placed her hand on Morgana, and Morgana could feel a strange tingling sensation that could only mean she was being put under a spell. Sure enough, she perceived a strange shift in the air around her, and it seemed that she was viewing the world from behind a veil.

'Quick,' said Esther, tugging at Morgana as she stood blinking her eyes trying to bring her surroundings back into focus. 'My invisibility spells never last long.'

She dragged Morgana back towards the fence just as two men in grey overalls appeared. Morgana could tell from Esther's nervous glances over her shoulder that she didn't quite trust her own spell-work, but neither of the men looked their way – that is, until Morgana walked straight into an already teetering pile of screws and bolts. They cascaded down in a metallic shower, pinging and clinking on the surrounding metal scraps.

'Who did that?' shouted the man named Igor, striding forward.

'It could have just fallen by itself,' said the first man, though he sounded unsure even as he suggested this, and joined Igor in his hunt amongst the mounds. He was standing just half a metre away from where the girls were crouching when he spoke again. 'Perhaps we should raise an alarm, just in case.'

This was all the girls needed to unfreeze them from their current state. They rose wordlessly and tried to creep silently towards the fence, but they couldn't avoid disturbing the debris that now littered the entire ground.

'There's something there!' called one of the men. Morgana looked down and could see that they were starting to flicker back into view. 'Call the security robots!'

Morgana and Esther abandoned their attempts at stealth and tore towards the fence, sending more rubbish crashing down around them. Though the men couldn't see the girls, the noise was impossible to miss. But the men seemed, for a moment, too alarmed at these ghostly apparitions to follow them, and the girls managed to slip back out through the fence and sprint away.

As they neared one of the great columns, their pace was slowed as they encountered a crowd waiting for a lift. Morgana drew to a halt. The invisibility spell was wearing off now, the misty veil around the two girls thinning.

'Let's join them,' she said. 'It'll be harder to find us among all these people.'

'Try not to sound too excited,' said Esther. But she stopped next to her, and they moved closer into the crowd as the spell disappeared completely.

Morgana's fear was swallowed by anticipation as the lift doors sprang open. She had never ridden in one before, never having had the money to pay the toll. Esther had always refused to try and sneak on before. The crowd inside disembarked and they were bundled forward into the tubes as the others waiting surged inside. The two small additional bodies went unnoticed in the crush.

Morgana couldn't help feeling a little under-whelmed by the new experience as the doors opened again almost as soon as they had closed, and the crowd spilt forth. Morgana could see the neat roads and respectable buildings of the second level just beyond, but just as they set foot outside, they were swept back in by the next group coming aboard and shooting upwards once again. The air was getting scarce and hot, and Morgana was now decidedly not enjoying the trip.

'We have to get off now,' hissed Esther in her ear as they felt the lift slow to a halt. As Morgana turned to her, she could see why Esther sounded so nervous. A tall thin man in uniform was making his way around, scanning screens of some kind which people were holding out for him. He eyed the girls' cloaks suspiciously, and was clearly making his way towards them. But his searching gaze was interrupted as he was momentarily blinded in the sudden stream of sunlight from the opening doors, and the girls took their chance to race forward, not caring about who they pushed aside in their hurry to get away.

Once they were clear of their fellow travellers, they stopped to catch their breath, but the air was much thinner up here and Morgana kept gasping at the sights around them. She had never persuaded Esther to come up to these heights before.

'In here,' said Morgana, pulling Esther towards a glass dome structure. 'They have better air in these. It says so on my map of the city.' And indeed, once they had entered they could feel the richer air filling their lungs.

'Wow,' said Esther as she looked around her.

Morgana couldn't take in her surroundings for a moment, she was so taken aback by how awed Esther appeared. The dome contained a lush park, nourished by its pocket of air. The grass was a deep green, interspersed with flowerbeds containing every colour of flower imaginable, all bold and exotic-looking, in vibrant colours, with none of the gentle beauty of the forest flora. As well as the people ambling about the place, and the robot groundskeepers working busily, there was a variety of wildlife roaming through the grounds. A peacock sauntered by, proudly displaying his plumage, as monkeys screeched in the trees above their heads.

'Ugh, better watch out we don't get any droppings on us,' said Esther, stepping from beneath the branches.

'Don't worry,' said Morgana, inspecting the creatures more closely. 'They're robots. See their metallic bellies?'

A woman passing gasped in horror as she spotted the two girls. 'Witches!' she exclaimed, clasping the front of her neon-green dress. 'You shouldn't be here. These parks are for city residents only!'

They two girls simply looked at each other and ran.

'There's witches and warlocks about the place!' The woman sounded quite hysterical behind them. Suddenly everyone in the park was looking around for them.

'Ugh!' said one man in a silver smock. 'Catch the filthy creatures before they curse us!'

'In here,' said Morgana, spotting a shed camouflaged amongst some shrubbery. She pulled Esther towards it.

They burst in. There was a robot inside, tending

to what seemed to be a malfunctioning robotic deer. He didn't even look up at the girls' entrance, but remained bent diligently over the table on which the deer was laid out. The rest of the shed was a contrasting clutter of natural plant life and the hard glitter of spare parts for the rest of the park's inhabitants.

'Oh, look,' said Morgana. 'We can definitely find something for Kitty here.'

'Morgana! There are more pressing matters at hand! We have to get out of here, but I can't think how.'

'Well,' said Morgana, surreptitiously pocketing a chicken claw and turning her attention back to their immediate situation. 'You don't think a wheelbarrow could be any harder to get airborne than a bathtub, do you?' she asked, pulling forth a grimy old wheelbarrow from the corner.

'More magic? Do you really think that's a good idea?'

'Probably not, but I can't think of any other way to escape.'

The people from the park had obviously seen

them enter the shed, as they had now caught up with them and were banging furiously at the door.

'Get out of there, you freaks!'

'The security robots are on their way!'

That convinced Esther. They had encountered various security robots in their trips around the city, and they were generally very big, very strong and not very reasonable.

'Get in the barrow,' she commanded Morgana, as she noiselessly opened the window on the opposite side to the door.

You didn't argue with Esther when she used that tone. Morgana got in obediently, Esther climbing in the front once she had the exit route cleared. Almost as soon as she was seated the wheelbarrow began to tremble ferociously, and seconds later they were blasting out through the window at such speed that Morgana couldn't help crying out in alarm. Her shouts mingled with the furious curses from the city's inhabitants as they watched them fly across the park and smash through the glass door of the entrance.

'Are you OK?' Esther called back.

'I'm fine,' said Morgana, although she had a few scratches. 'Are *you* OK?' she asked, pulling some shards of glass from her friend's dark hair.

'I managed to get a bit of a protective shield up, so it could have been worse.'

They were now soaring above the city. People glanced their way, but no one seemed too worried. Morgana wondered if perhaps they took them for some new type of flying vehicle. Having – most likely – never before seen two young witches flying in a wheelbarrow, they didn't recognize them as magic folk.

Morgana didn't notice anything below them at first. She was too exhilarated by the flight. Her parents had taken her on quick spins in the woods, but to be up so high, with no trees hemming her in, was a different sensation. She had convinced herself she had no interest in flying, but this was incredible. She felt almost a part of the air. And to know Esther was in control of this was astounding. As she became used to the experience, she glanced below them, and saw that her friend was speeding them away from the city.

'Oh, Esther, can't we go for a quick ride around?' she asked. 'It all looks amazing from up here!'

'We're flying, Morgana. We could go anywhere in the world. See all that nature has to offer. Visit far-flung magic communities. Go to the wilderness to try and find the last of the dragons. But you just want to see the city from a different angle?'

'Well . . . yeah,' said Morgana. 'I mean, I won't ever have the chance again, seeing as you're not coming down with me any more,' she added into the stony silence.

'Oh, all right, then,' said Esther. 'But just quickly.'

They dropped down to the second level, where the air was easier to breathe, and did a quick tour around the city's circumference. Morgana tried to imagine what might be happening in all the buildings they passed over. One was easy enough to guess at: 'School,' she read out loud from the sign above the gate, watching the children mingling with robots in the yard behind the building. 'What do you suppose they actually do in those places?'

'Learn all about those robots, and whatever other technology they use, I guess,' said Esther.

Morgana sat in stunned silence as Esther took them back to the mountainside. She had never really thought much about what school actually entailed. From the way they were warned about what to do during education inspections, it always made it seem like they were simply places where city folk learnt to hate magic folk. But perhaps not. Perhaps she really could learn all about robots! Perhaps the answer to all her dreams had been bursting into her home at regular intervals and she had been running away and hiding from it.

Well, not any more.

Chapter Five

Morgana thought she had her mind made up, but still the doubt crept in when she next heard the racket of the education inspectors' approach. She was deep in the woods, letting Kitty test out her new leg at a safe distance from the village. She could hear the other kids running in her direction, away from the inspectors. Did she really have the strength to walk against that tide?

Kitty gave her a nudge, probably more for attention than as encouragement. Morgana still took some strength from it, and strode forward. There was rustling in the branches overhead as legs disappeared into the foliage.

'What are you doing?' said Turlough, appearing from one of the trees. His mane of brown curls was even wilder than usual, his rosy cheeks flushed with rage. 'You know the rules. Get back here now!'

Morgana acted like she had heard nothing. Her resolve was too fragile to listen to others; she just had to follow her instinct and carry on. So she hurried forward through the trees, ignoring the chattering above her head as the other children from the village began calling to her, and then tried to work out what was happening among themselves when she refused to answer.

The confused voices were growing quite loud by the time Morgana reached the clearing. She could see one of the inspectors glancing back nervously towards the trees, perhaps wondering whether he could pretend he didn't hear the din. She smiled, suddenly feeling sure of her plan: she would make sure she wasn't so easy to ignore.

'Here I am!' she cried, bursting forth from the trees.

Almost as one, every jaw around her went slack, and she felt the eyes of every witch, warlock and inspector looking at her in disbelief.

Morgana began to feel embarrassed by her dramatic entrance under all these staring eyes. Was it too late to slink back into the woods? But then, without a word exchanged between them, the inspectors all turned their backs and began to walk away.

'Nothing here!' one of them said, which was their usual signal to leave.

'Wait!' cried Morgana, finding her determination again now that things weren't going to plan. 'I'm right here, and I'm not nothing.'

She raced in front of the man leading the group, but he kept going as though she was invisible. He tried to sidestep her, but Morgana was too quick for him. He then made to escape the other way, but again she was in his path. As he turned from her once more, he was in such a hurry to get away that he didn't notice Kitty darting under his feet. He tripped right over her, toppling face forward on to the ground. Rolling on to his back, spitting out a handful of leaves, he couldn't ignore Morgana any longer as she stood over him, smiling down.

'I think you're looking for me.'

'I'm looking for nothing,' he said gruffly, getting up and brushing the dirt off his uniform. 'I'm especially not looking for trouble.'

'Nor are we,' said Morgana's father, grabbing her by the hood of her cloak and starting to drag her away towards their cabin. Morgana wriggled free.

'Well, if you're not looking for trouble, then I think it best you don't break any of the laws you're employed to enforce,' she said, planting herself firmly before the inspector once more, hands on hips. 'I am a child who has never been to school, and I am quite determined to go. So what are you going to do about it?'

'Are you threatening me, child?' he said, looming over her.

Morgana resisted the urge to scurry away, ignoring the fear in her mother's voice as she called to her. She didn't answer the inspector, but stood as tall as she could, not breaking eye contact. It was the inspector who slumped first, looking around helplessly, clearly not entirely sure what the next stage of his job was.

'Well, I suppose we should . . .' He trailed off.

Luckily, help was at hand. One of the other inspectors stepped forward eagerly. He was much younger than the rest of them, with a slight dusting of acne about his cheeks. His uniform was clean and pressed, unlike those of his colleagues, and he was carrying an official-looking satchel from which he produced some documents. He cleared his throat and began to read from one of them.

'Under the Truancy Act, I am obliged to inform you that, having been found to have a child under the age of sixteen not enrolled in formal education, you are now under caution from the Department of Education. You must complete and return these forms within the next five working days.' He paused for breath, thrusting some papers into Morgana's father's hands before continuing: 'You will then be informed in writing of the school the child will attend and their start date. Failure to comply with the above and ensure the child attends school on a regular basis will lead to prosecution and a possible custodial sentence.'

Here his speech finished. Without written instruction on how to behave any more, he simply shuffled away awkwardly, some of his co-workers sniggering as he did so.

'Well, you heard the man,' snarled the head inspector to Morgana's parents. He then stooped down to Morgana's eye level and, grabbing her shoulders, looked her full in the face. 'You'd better stay so keen to go to school. Because if I'm being sent chasing up these mountains after you when you've realized your little witch brains aren't cut out for it, then my visits are going to get a lot less friendly.'

He let go of her roughly and stormed off, the rest of his team following closely behind. His warning didn't stifle Morgana's elation, though, and nor did the dark stares of her neighbours. It was her father's refusal to look at her that took some of the momentum out of her rising joy.

'I'm sorry, Dad, but I just—'

He simply turned to walk into the woods, still not looking at her as he spoke:

'I curse the day I took you down to that city.'

Chapter Six

Over the week following the education inspection, Morgana had to keep reminding herself that she was about to get everything she had ever wished for, and that she should be happier than ever, but sadness kept slipping in as she felt the distance growing between her and her family. Her mother was trying to act like everything was normal, but all their conversations felt strained, and when they spoke school was never mentioned. She stopped asking Morgana to attend her magic lessons, which ought to have been a relief, but really made her feel more left out than ever. To her father Morgana simply didn't exist any more. He couldn't even bring himself to look at her. It was only Turlough who had no problem speaking his mind.

'You have betrayed us all. And not just the family, but the whole magic community.'

The first time he had expressed similar sentiments it had hurt Morgana deeply. Her brother had always been very serious, pestering her to improve her magic, but he had never been hateful towards her like this. But having heard his little speech about seventeen times now, Morgana could do little but roll her eyes. Also, she suspected he was partly in a bad mood because of the very annoyed pig sitting beside him. His latest attempt to win over a familiar was not going well.

'You can still live the life you want here in the woods, Turlough, and I can live mine down in the city. It's my choice, it doesn't affect anyone else.'

'Doesn't affect anyone else?! It's breaking our parents' hearts. *And* bringing shame on our family. Do you know how it looks to the rest of the community? You turning your back on our way of life?'

Morgana assumed it didn't look very good, given how everyone else in the village was treating her. Most of them seemed to think she was afflicted with some terrible plague, and stayed well out of her way, in case her desire to leave the woods was somehow catching. Still, she preferred these people staying out of her way to those who kept tracking her down to tell her exactly what they thought of her.

It was only Esther who treated Morgana the same as she had always done.

'Well, you certainly have shaken up these woods,' she said laughingly, flopping down beside Morgana as she lounged with Kitty by the stream. No longer having to hide Kitty had brought Morgana some comfort over the past days. She and Esther were the only creatures in the woods who wanted to be anywhere near her. Even the cows had seemed quite cold towards her.

'I'm telling you, Morgana, you're the only thing that anyone can talk about at the moment,' continued Esther.

'I have a feeling they're not saying anything good.'

'No, I'm afraid it's mostly negative, and very boring. I only came to find you because I thought you might be the one person in these woods who doesn't want to discuss Morgana Mage.'

And she was right. So instead they talked about everything else. How they were lacking space in their den, and would need to expand soon, how it was Mrs Murphy's turn to cook for the village tonight and everyone was worried after the explosion of bodily fluids that had followed her last culinary attempts, and how Turlough was sick with jealousy over the incredibly powerful wind enchantment Esther had produced yesterday. By the time they were making their way back to the village Morgana had almost forgotten how unwelcome she was there. The stony face of her father quickly reminded her, though.

'We've just received notice,' he said. 'You start school on Monday.'

He then turned away instantly, returning

Morgana to her state of invisibility, though she hardly noticed. Now that she had a fixed date, she realized that this was really happening. Her dream was about to begin, and she was in a sudden state of euphoria that would continue over the following days. Esther could no longer turn to her for a break from the talk of her enrolment. Morgana was very grateful for her patience, as there was no one else who even remotely shared her enthusiasm, but Esther seemed to delight in her friend's barely contained joy.

'I wonder if the robots will be teaching us, or will it be people teaching us how to use robots? Or even make robots! Could you imagine if one day I could create a robot of my own?'

'What? Like a second Morgana? I don't think the world is ready for that. One is more than enough.'

'It wouldn't have to be like me at all,' said Morgana. 'In fact, you'll be glad to know I would make a number of improvements. I would create a robot that would do everything better than me, so I wouldn't have to do anything at all.'

She leant back, resting her head on her arms, smiling at the thought of this leisurely future.

'So, you would put so much time and effort into creating something that could do everything better than you, instead of just learning to do things yourself? I don't understand this technological world at all.'

'You could, though, Esther! With your brains you could understand anything you put your mind to. Turlough spends so much time learning spells that come so easily to you. I'm sure that if you came with me you would end up one of the greatest robot builders of the age.'

'My mind is for magic, though, that is where my gift lies. I'll leave the technology to you.'

'Still, though, I wish you were coming with me,' said Morgana, feeling the first twinge of regret at the thought of leaving her friend behind.

Mum woke her in the morning. 'Come on, love, time to get ready for school.'

Normally there was no getting Morgana out of bed while it was still dark out, but she sprang up straight away. The look of horror on her parents' faces as she arrived down to breakfast couldn't even quench her excitement.

'What are you wearing?' asked her mother.

'I made it myself,' Morgana answered proudly, giving them a twirl.

She was still wearing her usual rough-spun trousers, and a linen shirt, but she had created a type of chain-mail vest made from a collection of metal bolts and eyelets she had gathered on her trips to the city. Her sturdy boots, too, had been studded with bits of metal, and her chestnut curls, gathered into a wild bun atop her head, were adorned with some of what she considered her most beautiful pieces of scrap.

'Well, at least that covers it a bit,' said her mother, as Morgana pulled on her heavy cloak to protect her from the autumnal morning chill.

'Well, I like it,' said Morgana, grabbing a piece of toast.

'I've made you a potion to calm your nerves as well,' said her mother, pressing a small vial into Morgana's hand.

'I'm not nervous,' she lied, slipping it in her pocket anyway.

'Best be going,' her father said, standing up. 'We've a fair way to go.'

So they set off. Morgana thought she saw a few faces peering out at them from other cabins, and from the looks of them they shared her parents' opinion of her new style. She swept her cloak a bit further off her shoulder so they could get a better view of her handiwork.

Kitty was safely tucked away in her satchel. Morgana felt that pets probably weren't allowed in school, but there was no way she was leaving her behind. Silently they trudged down the mountain-side. The sky was beginning to lose its inky consistency, lightening to a misty purple with an orange glow spreading along the horizon just visible through the trees.

'Pay attention, now,' said her father as the trees around them began to thin out and the ground lost some of its steepness. 'I won't be able to come with you every morning. If you're determined to go to school you're going to have to make your own way there.'

Morgana nodded and looked away quickly. She always hated lying to her parents, and knew they would be horrified if they knew about her secret trips.

Eventually, they reached the city and made their way down a broad tree-lined street on the second level. Huge buildings reached up to tickle the underside of the top level of the city. The streets were busier than Morgana had ever seen them, and became busier still as they passed one of the columns and a lift popped open beside them to release its morning masses. As she was studying the crowd, trying to figure out where everyone might be off to, she crashed into her father, who had stopped before one of the buildings.

'Here we are,' he said. 'Bit of a trek to get to, though apparently it's the closest school to us. But a simple enough journey. You'll have no trouble finding the way.'

Morgana didn't hear any of this as she stood staring in wonder at the building before her. Set a bit back from the street, it wasn't the tallest building around, but it seemed very grand. Grey stone made up the archway of its entrance, as well as tracing the bottom of the building and the roof. The rest of it was a pure and glistening glass, catching the morning light. Morgana could just about make out the shadows of figures hurrying within. The stone roof was topped off with a great glass dome, reflecting the flashes of students arriving by teleportation. Those arriving by more conventional means pushed past her to get through the stone columns that stood guarding the drive.

'Well, I'd best be off.'

Morgana was suddenly very aware of her father once more, now that he was about to leave her. She looked at him with wild panic, and for the first time in what felt like an age he looked her directly in the eye.

'Good luck,' he said, pulling her into a quick hug. 'I'll see you back in the woods.'

And then he was gone, and Morgana was standing in front of what she supposed was still her dream, though right now it was filling her with so much dread and terror that it felt more like a nightmare.

Chapter Seven

Morgana stuck her hand in her satchel to remind herself that she still had Kitty by her side. Kitty gave her a reassuring nudge. Morgana inhaled deeply and took off at a quick march down the drive.

Moments before, all the other students had seemed completely oblivious to her presence as they almost stampeded over her to get through the gates, but now they turned as one to gawp at her.

Morgana wasn't surprised at their stares. Despite her attempt to make her outfit more city-like, she still stood out sharply in this crowd of metallic and neon clothes, all made out of strange materials she felt sure her mother couldn't enchant her wheel to spin. While Morgana had put a bit more effort into her hairstyle than usual, she couldn't be entirely sure that the geometric shapes sported by every head around her were even made of hair. Certainly, her dusting of freckles couldn't compete with the metallic powder swept over eyelids, the glittering patterns etched on some of the cheeks, and the lips of blue and orange. The only colour in Morgana's face was the red she could feel rising under the force of a thousand staring eyes. She didn't turn to meet these stares. She just kept walking forward, head held high, up to the doors of the school.

As soon as she passed over the threshold, she lost all sense of purpose and found herself standing frozen just inside the entrance. She realized that she had no idea where to go, or what she was supposed to do. How did schools even work? If there had been any instructions in the letter her parents had received, they hadn't mentioned it.

There was a row of lifts before her, shooting up and down between the floors, and the corridors to either side of the great hall she was standing in were leading to glass-walled rooms where students were beginning to congregate.

Morgana found herself wishing she was at home. It may not be perfect, but at least home was safe and familiar. Her heart was already pounding with anxiety when a sudden loud ringing of bells almost sent it bursting clear out of her chest. She figured this was some sort of signal, as everyone from outside came pouring in through the doors, once more completely unaware of Morgana in their haste. The crowd around her was so dense that she could hardly see, and she was having trouble catching her breath when, as suddenly as they had all come surging in, everyone was gone again, like a wave retreating after crashing on the shore. Morgana was left standing on her own.

A brief feeling of calm descended on her, before she was consumed by panic. Her instinct was telling her to turn around and head back to the mountains. But how could she explain to everyone that she had barely made it past the door before giving up on everything she had ever wanted? So, she made a decision and took a determined turn to the right down the nearest corridor. She was simply going to have to find someone and ask her way.

The corridors were deserted, so she decided she would need to knock on one of the doors. She was trying to decide which one looked the least intimidating when a figure glided out in front of her. Two metres of polished metal, a body made of a great square with a smaller cube on top, from which came a soothingly inhuman voice.

'What is your business in this school? I have no record of your DNA in my student or staff files.'

'No, well, it's my first day here today. But I was told to come. I got a letter . . .' She trailed off, realizing she didn't have the letter with her. Perhaps she would have to return to the woods after all . . . but then she noticed the glowing eyes of the robot were flashing.

'Yes, the files show a new student was due to register today. Are you Morgana Mage?'

'Yes, that's me.'

'Please follow me to the administration offices.'

Morgana trotted behind the robot, which moved quite elegantly and swiftly despite its chunky body seeming too large for its thin metal legs. As she watched it walk before her she was reassured that she was doing the right thing being here. Yes, everything was strange and new, but she would never understand the wonder in front of her if she stayed up in the mountains for ever.

'Please enter here for processing,' said the robot, opening a door at the end of the corridor. Morgana stepped past him into a white room with another, rectangular robot standing stationary in the middle.

'Please stand in front of me,' the second robot said. Morgana did as she was told. 'Stand straight,' it commanded, and Morgana obeyed. 'I shall take a scan of your face and a sample of your DNA so the school infrastructure will be able to recognize you.'

A rod popped out from the top of the robot, emitting a glow of blue light as it passed before her face, then the light dimmed and the rod shot forward to pinch the top of her finger.

'Ow!' said Morgana, more from surprise than actual pain.

She was warier when a second instrument emerged from the machine, a metal semi-circle that attached itself to her temples. She could feel it sending slight vibrations through to her skull.

'Following a reading of brain activity, I assign you to class 1A. Here is a hard copy of your timetable, as I can detect no capable electronic device about your person.'

Morgana thought she could feel Kitty shuffle indignantly in her bag.

A piece of paper slid from the bottom of the machine. Morgana just managed to catch it before it hit the floor.

'Please report to class.'

She was very disappointed upon leaving the room to find that the first robot had deserted her, so instead she turned to the timetable to guide her. It looked like she now had history in class-room 4.3 on the fourth floor. She made her way back to the entrance hall, and after much trouble over the workings of the buttons on the lift – resulting in a trip to the basement, followed by a jaunt up to the roof – she eventually found herself on the fourth floor. She paused to collect herself in front of the door marked 4.3, before pushing it open and taking her first timid steps inside a classroom. Thirty pairs of eyes looked up at her, wide in shock.

Is this room 4.3?' asked Morgana anxiously, glancing from her timetable to the number on the door.

The look of disbelief on the teacher's face had her doubting the navigation skills she'd been so proud of just moments before. He walked over to her, snatching up her timetable.

'You're the witch child, I suppose . . . the administration robot ran the usual tests on you, did it?' he asked, frowning as he studied the sheet.

'Well, they didn't feel very usual to me,' she said. 'But yes, I guess so.'

The teacher looked at her blankly, then appeared to pull himself together.

'Well, I suppose you should take a seat, then. I'm Mr Harris.'

Morgana moved to sit beside a pretty girl at the front of the class with blonde hair twisted into a cone on the top of her head, but the girl shoved her bag on to the unoccupied seat. 'Don't even think about it,' she snarled, eyes narrowed. The girls behind her laughed. Both of them were also beautiful, one with her hair in a brilliant afro, the other with her flaming hair twisted in plaits around her skull.

Morgana jumped back as if stung. The teacher was about the same distance away from the girls, but if he had heard the remark, he made no reaction.

She looked around the classroom. There were a couple of other tables with single occupants, but she thought it safest to make for the empty table down the back. She settled down in the corner, feeling safely out of the way, when the boy in front with spiked black hair raised his hand.

'Sir,' he practically shouted, 'I really don't think I can concentrate here with, you know' – here he paused to glance back at Morgana – 'the smell.'

The girls at the front giggled again. Morgana could feel the anger rise brightly to her cheeks. She knew any smell coming from her could only be pleasant. Her clothes were freshly laundered, and she had had her daily bath with rosewater and lavender the night before. She looked to the teacher for support in her indignation, but he didn't seem to notice her at all.

'Well, find another desk, then, Mr Zhang,' he said, gesturing about the room.

'He can sit here, sir,' said the blonde girl, removing her bag from the chair beside her.

'Perfect. There beside Clodagh, Henry.'

'Sir?' asked Clodagh as Henry sat beside her. 'There are some magic people who haven't moved to the woods still in the Undercity. I know these types of people don't need, or want, an education, but couldn't some sort of schools be built down there, so we don't have our learning disrupted?'

'Well,' said Mr Harris, still acting as though Morgana wasn't in the room, 'I don't think a situation like this has arisen before. Hopefully it'll sort itself out in time.'

'Yes, well, I certainly will be saying something to my father,' said Clodagh. 'The mayor,' she added for Morgana's benefit.

Morgana stared at the table in front of her, not blinking in case she disturbed the tears brewing behind her eyes. She could feel the black boy with the tightly shaved head at the table next to her looking her way, but she didn't have the strength to meet the gaze of what she assumed to be another contemptuous face. Kitty must have sensed her despair, as she poked out a metallic claw to scratch her a friendly reminder that she had one friend close by.

Morgana only raised her head again to look about helplessly when the teacher announced that everyone should put on their virtual reality headsets to tour the battlefields of the Intercity Robot War. The rest of the class snapped on some neat-looking goggles and popped something in their ears. Morgana found herself jealous to be missing out on the horrors that they seemed to be experiencing, as they screamed and even wept over whatever visions were before them, while she never left the classroom. Everyone returning from this spectacle of war still seemed to finish the lesson in a brighter mood than she did. Morgana was hopeful at least that the rest of her classes must be better than this.

She was wrong. The next class was maths, where Ms Mulcahy talked to her like her mother talked to foreign witches and warlocks who visited the woods – very slowly and very loudly.

'TODAY WE ARE STUDYING AL-GE-BRA.'

Almost blown away by her teacher's volume, Morgana went to take her seat at the back of the classroom, as everyone else seemed to be sitting in a similar formation to the class before. At least Morgana didn't feel completely left out of the class this time, as she could follow some of the formulas on the screen at the front, having started learning algebra with her mother.

This didn't last long, though, as shortly into the class the teacher asked them to take out their scrolls. Morgana was bewildered. Surely they didn't use the parchment still favoured by some of the older magic folk? Then she realized that the rest of the students were already unrolling their scrolls, and the reason she hadn't noticed was that these scrolls were barely visible. They were as clear as glass, but as thin and pliable as paper.

Ms Mulcahy began swiping some of the problems on the screen towards the students. Morgana could see them disappear from the screen at the top of the class and then pop up on the scrolls around her. As they finished the problems the students would send them back to the class screen with a flick of the wrist. At first Morgana was so mesmerized by the disappearance and reappearance of numbers that she didn't think to feel neglected, but she became quite frustrated when she realized that she could have provided better answers than some of those flying through the air, if only she could get involved.

Lunchtime was another struggle. As she lined up for her food, she noticed that everyone was standing a good metre away from her on either side. When she reached the top of the queue, she couldn't recognize any of the foodstuffs in front of her. They just looked like a variety of chewy-looking lumps in different shades of beige. It all looked so unappetizing that she almost turned and left without anything, but then a robot arm appeared from behind the counter and performed a scan of her. It then picked up one of the nondescript blobs and placed it on her tray.

'This meal is pleasing to your taste buds and will fit your required nutrient profile,' the robot said in its tinny voice.

Morgana didn't argue but carried her tray to the quietest table in the canteen, which emptied completely once she sat down. Surprisingly, the food didn't taste awful, but nor did it feel quite like food, although she felt full and energized for her next class.

Her participation was once again impossible, however, as the music teacher, Ms Roberts – who seemed terrified of Morgana – asked everyone to put their earbuds in to listen to the piece they were learning. After that they all put on their goggles to practise their virtual instruments. Morgana had to sit in silence, doing her best to ignore the nervous glances Ms Roberts was casting her way. When she did meet her eye once, the teacher turned a deathly pale and had to clutch on to her desk to prevent herself from fainting away.

Morgana was relieved she wouldn't have to deal with any similar nonsense in her final class of the day. Robotics was indeed taught by a robot, who treated her with the same cool demeanour it used for the rest of the class. She delighted in watching her teacher open its own body to discuss how its innards worked, and couldn't help asking every question that popped into her head, regardless of the laughter they usually brought forth from the rest of the class. The teacher, Instructor 1107 as it was called, answered everything matter-of-factly, with absolutely no judgement.

Still, though, this detached and professional attitude couldn't counteract the active hostility Morgana had faced from everyone else, and she was shocked that when the end-of-day bell rang, she was actually happy to leave this robot behind and make her way back to the woods. She may not fit in there either, but there were a few people who didn't mind.

Chapter Eight

Morgana's days followed a similar pattern for the rest of the week. Forcing herself to get up every morning, she would dress in the dark. She had thought she might abandon her new style, but realized that even if no one else was impressed with her fashions, *she* still loved them. So, tinkling lightly as she walked, she would set off on the long trip to school. Here she would be met by the cold stares and cruel words of her classmates. The teachers could be just as bad, with even more subtly snide remarks, or else treating her like a complete idiot, yet offering her no actual help with her learning.

Ironically, it was only her robot teachers – there was one for science as well as robotics – that treated her with any humanity. To them she was just another student, and Morgana always looked forward to these lessons for this reason, as well as the close proximity to robots. It was just a pity the other students were still there as well.

'So,' Morgana asked Instructor 1107, trying to get a grasp of the basics. 'The robot will take different kinds of sensory input from their surroundings, then this is all processed in the central processing unit. The robot will have been programmed so that depending on the type of sensory input it will know what to do.'

'Yes, that is a simple overview.'

'God, imagine having no idea of such basic robotics,' said Henry in the loudest possible excuse for a whisper.

Morgana felt herself colour, but the robot arm Henry and Clodagh were working on was remaining stubbornly still, while Jonathan, the boy at the desk next to Morgana, had managed to get *his* robot drawing his portrait. Morgana decided it wouldn't be Henry she turned to for an assessment of her robotics skills.

The classes where Morgana was embarrassed by her lack of understanding were still better than those where she couldn't participate at all. She sat in silence while Mr Ali whisked the class to the theatre and everyone laughed around her, sat idle in geography as Ms Connolly fitted all their scrolls together to make a map of the country created by everyone except Morgana, and missed out on countless other sights and sounds she was completely unaware of.

She felt that it was a kind of insanity brought on by extreme boredom that caused her to utter the stupidest possible thing in history class.

'Magic?'

'What did you say?' said Mr Harris, glaring at her from across the classroom, his eyes bulging. They were studying the Inter City Robot War still, and he had asked what had brought it to an end. It had never occurred to Morgana that they might have a different version of events, but she really should have known better than to utter that word in these surroundings. Then, to fill the threatening silence that was now surrounding her, she spoke of the witches and warlocks revealing themselves to come to the aid of the city and save it from destruction.

'Are these the kind of lies your people tell?' roared Mr Harris in a rage, before she had even finished. 'Trying to take from the glorious history of our city and invent a noble history for your people in the process. I can't even look at you, you despicable creature. Get out of my classroom! OUT!'

Morgana raced out as fast as she could. It was the last class of the day, but she didn't want to have to explain an early return to the forest, so she hid in the bathroom, with Kitty, who had been released from her hiding place to cuddle up to her, absorbing some of her tears with her sparse fur.

Morgana was always afraid of Kitty being discovered. It had never been explicitly stated, but she could guess from the lack of any other pet in the school that they weren't allowed. She couldn't bring herself to leave Kitty at home, though, or her loneliness would have been too complete. Kitty always remained safely concealed during class, but after Morgana had gulped down a lonely lunch, she could usually find an empty classroom or bathroom to spend a few moments of companionship with her pet. Although Kitty was more than a pet – Morgana really did see her as a familiar now.

She thought she might have been able to cope better with the misery of her school life if she could have found some comfort at home. But, too proud to admit she may have made a bad decision, she returned to the woods after her first day beaming from ear to ear, ready to tell anyone who would listen how incredible her school was. After that, she felt she would have to keep up the charade, but it was so difficult to lie to her family and Esther. She had always been honest with them before, and they knew her so well she felt sure they would see through her façade if they dug even a little way beneath the surface of her cheery exterior.

So she began to keep her distance. Pretending

she was doing homework, though she didn't have the technology or the technological skills to manage any of it, she spent most of her evenings on her own, retreating further into her lonely silence. On the first weekend she hid away in the den by the river. She was simply gazing at her old map, part of her wishing she had kept the city as a fantasy on a wall, when Esther popped her head around their door. Morgana was shocked to feel her heart drop at the sight of her best friend.

'Surely you can't still be doing homework,' she said brightly. 'You must have a whole robot army built by now.'

'I've a lot to learn before then,' grumbled Morgana. 'It's not as simple as magic.'

'Ha! When have you ever found magic simple?'

Morgana felt a deep sadness wash over her, but it was tinged with a biting anger. Usually she was happy to join Esther in laughing at her lack of magic abilities, but it felt different now. Esther's joke stung badly now that Morgana was beginning to feel she might not have the talents to prosper anywhere in this world.

'Ugh, I just can't talk to you about any of this stuff,' she snapped. 'You don't understand anything beyond these woods. You're just as ignorant as everyone else here.'

Esther's mouth hung open wide in shock, then her face fell into a furious scowl. 'You're not better than us, Morgana, just because you're a city girl now.'

'Ha!' laughed Morgana, thinking of how ridiculous the idea of her being a city girl was.

Esther obviously thought the laugh was directed at her, as her anger only intensified.

'Well, fine then. It's clear you don't need your old friends any more. You've hardly said a word to me since you started school. I knew you couldn't wait to leave these woods. I just didn't realize that I was part of what you wanted to get away from.'

Esther's eyes began to fill with tears, and she turned and stormed away. Morgana wanted to say something to stop her, but her own tears had a stranglehold on her.

She didn't want to face anyone else that night, but knew no one else would visit her in the den. She could be alone with her metal. As she settled in among her piles of it, she immediately began to feel calmer, but her frustrations began to grow again as she realized that there was nothing that she could do with this by herself. She had none of the tools from the workshops in school, and her friend's fire power wasn't available to her now. She eyed up the jars of fire Esther had collected around the place, with their different coloured flames all burning brightly.

She toyed with the lid of a small purple inferno. It was only a small jar, but she didn't think she would need much heat to shape this particular metal. She prised the lid off slowly, but the moment it was slightly open a bright flame jumped forth. Morgana shut the lid again, tightly, but there was no way to get the fire back in. It crackled menacingly in the middle of the floor. Morgana normally only had to look at the campfire in the village and it would go out, but this was rising up to meet her.

'Oh no, oh no!' she murmured. Looking around desperately, she noticed a cauldron full of bright green liquid.

Morgana paused for a moment. Despite the hours she had spent with Esther, watching her brew her concoctions, she had absolutely no idea what it might be. For all she knew it could be some special brew designed to grow a fire. Deciding to take a chance anyway, she tipped it over. It landed right on top of the flames, which were extinguished immediately, but left behind an acrid thick red smoke that stank of rotten meat and burning hair. Morgana rushed outside. Who knew what effects the combination of the spell and the potion might create?

She coughed a deep hacking cough as she slumped against the wall of the den, feeling even more useless than before. It took her a moment to notice that the shaft of metal she had been hoping to reshape was still clasped in her hand. Morgana's frustration began to shift into rage. She knew exactly what she wanted to do with the piece of metal, but all the various means of achieving it were beyond her. Everyone else had some power over the world around them, but she was just completely helpless. It wasn't fair. Anyone else would be able to twist this metal . . .

She stopped in her thoughts. The smoke must be having some effect on her. She was seeing things: the metal was curving. Morgana blinked back the tears from the smoke and annoyance still blurring her vision. But it couldn't be. How? She must be imagining it. She was so shocked that it took her a moment to notice the heat spreading through the metal. She dropped the piece of metal, which was now bent into a C shape. The red marks on her hands were definitely real enough.

She raced back to the village, exhilarated but confused. It had probably been some effect from the potion and the flames, she reasoned. It couldn't have been her. Yes, that made more sense.

She hardly slept at all that night. Realizing that it must have been Esther's powers that had been the cause after all, she was left again picturing the pain on the face of her friend, as well as dreading the day that faced her when she went back to school in the morning.

Chapter Nine

Morgana rose with the dawn, still worrying about Esther. Not only did she not have any friends in school, but now she was ruining her other friendships too. She got ready quite unthinkingly. What was the point in trying to look presentable when everyone was just going to act like she was smelly and dirty anyway? So she pulled on her boots without bothering to scrape off the muck, and barely tried to wrestle a comb through her unruly curls. She still refused to abandon her newly-fashioned armour, though.

She then tramped along the now-familiar path down the mountainside and into the city. As cars zipped over her head and robots glided by her, she found that even these marvels couldn't distract her from the gnawing anxiety she could feel in the pit of her stomach as she approached the school building. At least she didn't have to face so many staring eyes now – this was partly just because her novelty had worn off, but also seemed to be a new tactic for those who wanted her to know how unwelcome she was still.

Clodagh and her gang strode past, heads in the air, looking anywhere but in Morgana's direction. Perhaps this was because they genuinely didn't notice her, but Morgana doubted this, as Clodagh managed to bump into her with such force that she was sent flying on her backside. Clodagh was still looking straight ahead, but it did bring the attention of everyone else in the yard back to Morgana. She tried to ignore the sniggers as she got up, brushed herself off and made her way to class, not paying any heed to the wide berth everyone gave her in the lift.

She kept her head down when she reached the classroom and made straight for her empty desk in the corner. When she sat down, she was so intent on keeping her eyes fixed on the floor that it took her a while to notice the figure standing in front of her. It was the tumble of gadgets on to her desk that brought her attention to Jonathan.

'I fixed these up for you over the weekend,' he said, arranging a scroll, some earbuds, and a rather chunky-looking pair of virtual reality goggles. 'Not the most up-to-date versions, I'm sure you can tell, but I've been able to tweak the software so they should keep up with the latest updates. In fact, I think I've made some marked improvements to the scroll. I showed my father and he said he'd pass some of my ideas on to the creators. He's one of the head engineers of RoboCorp, so he knows some of the guys in Scroll Inc. He also let me download some RoboCorp reading to your scroll. You've been asking some very incisive questions for someone who's only just encountering robotics. I think you'll find it interesting.'

Mr Harris slammed the door, sending Jonathan

scuttling back to his desk, where he had sat in silence all the previous week. It was Morgana who was now speechless as she toyed with the instruments before her. Before she could properly inspect them, Mr Harris began to bark instructions from the top of the classroom.

'Goggles on! Virtual reality again today. Much more ancient history, though – we are going back to the French Revolution.'

Morgana noticed he was unshaven and red-eyed. He seemed to prefer to let the virtual reality devices do the teaching when he looked like this. Morgana had noticed that he didn't mind having a snooze in front of her, but always waited until everyone else's goggles and earbuds were firmly in place before dozing off. Morgana was glad she wouldn't have to watch him dribbling today. She eagerly picked up her goggles before realizing that she didn't have any idea what to do with them, but before her heart had a chance to sink, Jonathan was sitting at her side.

'Hmmm, they might be a bit tight,' he said.

'No, no, they're perfect,' said Morgana, ignoring

the slight pinch.

'OK, well, I have them set up on the network, so there isn't much for you to do but wait for Mr Harris to send out the VR file.'

He had barely finished this sentence when Morgana suddenly found herself on the streets of eighteenth-century Paris. It was quite disconcerting at first to find herself in this jostling crowd of Parisians. She could feel the press of the crowd around her and could even smell the stench of them. In fact, the smell was so overpowering that it took her a while to notice the disembodied voice narrating the events taking place. Suddenly the scene changed, and Morgana was storming the barricades, adrenaline pumping through her veins. They were taken through a few more scenes before ending up in front of the guillotine. Despite how gruesome this bloody finish to the experience was, Morgana still felt herself smiling the whole way through it, knowing that back in the reality of the modern day she had a companion sitting by her side.

'Don't worry, I'll show you how to access it,'

Jonathan said as Mr Harris told them he would upload their homework to their scrolls, having abruptly cut off their VR feeds, looking like he had just woken from a deep slumber.

As they made their way to the next class of the day Jonathan rattled off all the features he had improved on Morgana's devices. 'The download speed is practically instantaneous, and I think the sound quality on your earbuds is even better than mine. I'm going to have to work on some upgrades for myself.'

Morgana just nodded along. Not knowing what half the features were, she was sure she wouldn't notice their enhancements, but nonetheless she was touched at the time and effort that had gone into making them. Still, she did begin to feel her eyes glaze over when Jonathan began to explain the science behind the changes he had made. She was pretty sure that even those who had grown up around all this technology would struggle to keep up with Jonathan, let alone someone who'd only been out of the woods for a week.

Morgana's suspicion was confirmed when she

asked if he was worried about missing his lessons, as he spent the whole of the maths class giving her a basic overview of how her scroll operated.

'Oh no,' said Jonathan, quite nonchalantly. 'I'm way beyond this level of mathematics.'

'I've done some of it before,' said Morgana. 'But I couldn't keep up without any of the technology.'

'Yes, I thought that. I couldn't stand how unfair it was. No one was even giving you a chance.'

'Well, you are now,' said Morgana. 'And I haven't even said thank you yet.'

'There's no need. I enjoy making things. Especially for someone who appreciates them. No one else in the class has ever known a life without technology, and they take it completely for granted. You're in awe of it in a way that few people are any more.'

'But you still are?' asked Morgana.

'I make a point of it,' he said proudly. 'You have to try and look at it with fresh eyes. It's the only way I'll be able to truly understand it, and then create even more amazing things. I want to take after my father. He has pushed the robotic age further and further through his work at Robo-Corp. I want to be a part of that some day.'

Morgana didn't feel bold enough to admit that she too would like to be a part of it, not when Jonathan was patiently trying to show her the simplest of functions on the most rudimentary of devices, but she tried to take in every word he said for the rest of the day. She was so captivated by all that she was learning that she couldn't believe it when the bell rang for the end of school, and was even more astounded to realize that for the first time in what felt like a long time, she was sorry to leave the city behind her.

Chapter Ten

Rarely had homework been done with such joy as Morgana completed hers that night, even if she was banished from the warmth of the cabin out to her den in the woods to do it. She had thought it best not to argue with Turlough when he was in one of his more self-righteous moods.

'I don't know how you have the audacity to bring that electronic filth into our home,' he snarled across the table as he copied out some potions from a book borrowed from elder Ms Garcia while she worked away on her scroll.

'Really, Turlough,' sighed Morgana. 'It's just another way of getting my homework done. I'm sure your fountain pen was quite revolutionary at one time. Shouldn't you be carving your work into a stone tablet or something?'

Turlough flung the pen down in a rage, splattering ink over the rough wooden walls of the cabin. 'My fountain pen doesn't go against all the traditions of our community. It's not going to destroy our way of life.'

Morgana knew he was in a particularly bad mood because his pig familiar had finally made its escape, disappearing up the mountains, but there was only so much she could handle. She made her own escape into the woods. She could read by the light of the scroll, but found herself wishing she could produce a fire spell once more as she shivered late into the night, until her mother came looking for her.

'Come in to bed, love. You'll have to be up in a few hours.'

Morgana followed her back home, but once she was sure that Turlough was asleep on his mattress at the other side of the cabin she had her scroll out under her covers. She just couldn't tear her eyes away from the new world it opened up to her. All those questions she was afraid to ask in class, she could type or even whisper into this glowing rectangle, and have the answers back in seconds.

She tried using the feature whereby placing some electrodes on her temples allowed her to communicate with it directly, but her mind was racing so much with everything she wanted to know that the device couldn't decipher it and politely asked if she would talk or type. In answer to her questions she was sent back text, sound and pictures to the screen – or even straight to her mind, when she tried the electrodes again – however, she found this experience so alarming that she tore the electrodes off as soon as the flood of information started to rush into her brain from the outside. Jonathan had told her that when you were sixteen you could even get a miniature scroll permanently embedded inside you, so that the flow of information could be constant. As much as Morgana loved technology, this seemed a slightly terrifying thought.

In the end she only got a couple of hours' sleep, and woke so exhausted that she doubted she could have ever torn herself from bed if she didn't know she had a friend waiting for her at the end of her morning journey.

As she walked into the classroom, she found Jonathan already sitting at the desk that had once been Morgana's own little island. He was waiting excitedly to explain some of the features he had enhanced even further on her machines. Morgana was excited to find she already recognized some of the words he was using, and was very pleased with herself for managing to get everything up and running by herself.

They again spent the morning crouched over these electronics, while the rest of the class carried on. By the time the bell rang for lunch Morgana had completely forgotten the rest of the world around them, but as they continued their discussions in the canteen it became clear that the rest of the world had still been very much aware of them.

'It's almost sweet that you've found each other,'

Clodagh said, leering down at them as she stood by their table with her tray, her henchmen Lisa and Claire giggling behind her as usual. 'Two of the biggest freaks in the school brought together.'

Morgana could feel her blood rising, but Jonathan looked at Clodagh calmly, not seeming the least bit bothered.

'You're such different kinds of freaks, though,' she continued. 'You're such a know-it-all, Jonathan, and this thing can barely speak.'

'Morgana is highly intelligent,' answered Jonathan serenely.

'Ha!' laughed Clodagh. 'She can barely turn her scroll on.'

Morgana could feel fury coursing through her, but for some reason she couldn't form that anger into words and put Clodagh in her place the way she always could with her brother, or any of the other kids in the woods who laughed at her for her terrible witchcraft.

'She has actually taken to the interfaces very quickly for someone who has only been using it for a day,' said Jonathan. 'If *you* had lived in the woods, cut off from technology, I think it would take you a lot longer to pick it up.'

'As if I would ever go near those disgusting woods,' she snarled. 'And I think you're a disgrace for encouraging this creature to come out of them, here, where she doesn't belong. I'm sure you know better than anyone that there was another mass malfunctioning of robots in the city last night. Well, everyone knows it's the witches' and warlocks' interfering that's causing these shut-downs. And here you are giving them more information about our technology – information they can then use to attack us.'

'There is no evidence that magic people have been involved in any of the recent technology issues,' said Jonathan.

'Sure,' said Clodagh. 'You just don't want to believe it because the only person who wants to be friends with you is a witch.' She made to walk away, then turned back as if she had forgotten to say something. 'Whoops!' She tipped her glass of bright red liquid straight into Morgana's lap.

Morgana jumped to her feet in shock, which

quickly turned to anger as the laughter erupted around her. She could feel her rage pulsating in her veins, bubbling to the surface as she turned to see Clodagh's smirking face. Clodagh still held her lunch tray, piled high with food. Morgana could tell it was made of stainless steel; she could almost sense it. It would be so easy to get her own back on Clodagh if she could only . . .

Before she had even finished that thought, the tray had flipped in the air, spilling its contents all down Clodagh's shimmering golden smock, then shot straight into Morgana's hand.

Morgana couldn't tell if the ear-splitting scream from Clodagh was more a scream of fury or of terror. It was answered by a wild yowling from her bag as Kitty seemed to sense a threat to Morgana, who could see her little furry ginger face peep through as she tried to free herself from her canvas prison. Morgana quickly bundled her away before she could be spotted, but she could tell from how freaked out everyone around her looked that they must have thought the noise came from her.

'I think we should go,' whispered Jonathan,

tugging her sleeve.

She gladly let him drag her to her feet and out into the school yard, where they sheltered behind some bins.

'Oh no, oh no!' she said, panic swelling in her chest. 'What have I done?'

'Given Clodagh exactly what she deserves,' answered Jonathan. 'That shriek, though – it didn't come from you, did it?' he asked, eyeing up her still-squirming bag.

Morgana didn't answer, but opened her satchel. Kitty came leaping out. Morgana snatched her up, holding her close to calm her. Eventually she was still enough for Jonathan to see something more than a streak of silver and orange.

'Wow, that's a really old-style robot pet. I've never seen such an ancient model. Though this looks like a new addition,' he said, touching her chicken-claw foot.

'She needed some patching up,' explained Morgana.

'You've done this yourself? I'm impressed. I mean, it's not very sophisticated, but it seems very effective, especially since I guess you were working with limited equipment and materials.'

'You can say that again.'

Kitty had obviously decided that Jonathan wasn't the source of danger she had picked up on, as she let him examine her more closely.

'Very few people bother even with robotic pets any more,' he said somewhat sadly, 'never mind real ones. Just too much hassle and taking up too much space. Most pets are virtual.'

'I can't imagine that's the same at all,' said Morgana, feeling her heart rate slow behind the comforting weight of Kitty pressed to her chest. Her mind had also stopped racing enough to allow her to think more clearly about what had just happened. 'What is it Clodagh thinks witches and warlocks are doing in the city, anyway?'

'Oh, there have been a lot of technological problems recently,' said Jonathan, his brow furrowed. 'Robots going haywire, refusing orders. No one is sure why any of it is happening, not even my father, so naturally you lot are getting the blame.'

'Great – so everyone hates magic folk more than

usual, and then I go and act more witchy than I ever have before. Why did I have to do magic?' she asked pleadingly, to herself more than Jonathan. 'I mean, I can't even *do* magic!'

'Then what was that?' asked Jonathan.

'I'm not sure. I mean, it *seemed* to be magic, but magic doesn't really work on metal, not like that. Though I did think I had some effect on it once before. But it couldn't have been. It doesn't make any sense.'

'I think there may be more magic to you than you think.'

'Well, I don't want it,' said Morgana. 'I don't need it. I want to use technology. Magic just makes life more difficult.'

'To be honest,' said Jonathan, 'no one here was ever going to accept you. So there was no point pretending that you're not a witch when no one else was going to let you forget it. At least they're afraid of you now. Just let on you're the greatest sorceress of the age. Keep Clodagh on her toes.'

They both laughed at this, but they did find that they were given quite a lot of space in the corridors as they made their way back to class. And when they got there most of the desks around theirs stood empty. However, as they saw it, this simply gave them a chance to carry on their own studies uninterrupted, and they were perfectly happy with that.

Chapter Eleven

Her school life now began to bring Morgana all the happiness she had hoped for. Every day Jonathan was teaching her new things about the world around her. The more she understood of the world, the more she felt a part of it, even if others were still trying to make her feel like she didn't belong.

'I know about your little stunt,' said Mr Harris one morning, leaning over their desk.

'Me, sir?' asked Jonathan, as Morgana sat dumb.

'You, Boyle?' said Mr Harris, looking surprised

Jonathan was even there. 'No, not you – what could *you* have done? I mean your little friend. Rumours have reached me that she was doing magic. Everyone seems to be afraid to report her, but if I get word of any more illegal activity, I will do everything in my power to have you out of this school.'

Morgana gulped as he stalked away.

'No need to worry,' said Jonathan. 'Just don't do any more magic.'

'Well, I couldn't even if I wanted to,' said Morgana. 'So that shouldn't be a problem.'

Even though she had said she didn't want to use magic – that technology was enough for her – she couldn't help trying it out. But the hours spent in the den trying to will her metal into shape hadn't produced any results.

Morgana did wonder why no one had put in a complaint, though. Surely it was just the opportunity they needed to get rid of her.

'They want to make sure they have more evidence first,' said Jonathan, when she asked him about it as they made their way to the next class.

'Look – everyone is just waiting to capture your next outburst.'

Morgana looked around her. Everyone was studiously avoiding eye contact, but she saw that lots of screens were facing her head-on. Some of the other students were trying to be inconspicuous with their scrolls, and had them folded up to mere centimetres, slotted into one of the many pockets that tended to adorn their clothes. Others had their scrolls fully unfolded and brazenly pointed towards her.

'I bet they're all disgusted they didn't get any footage of your last bit of sorcery for ScrollTown. I'm sure it would have been very popular.'

'Scroll what?' asked Morgana.

'ScrollTown. It's a virtual-reality hang-out space, you can share pictures and videos. I avoid it, though. Turns out these kids can be just as mean virtually as they are in real life. Another show from you would be bound to get them some of the attention they crave there.'

The music teacher had obviously heard about Morgana's display too: she trembled as Morgana entered, moving behind her desk for protection.

'Miss?' said Jonathan, with a knowing glance towards Morgana. 'Seeing as me and Morgana don't have much talent for music, we thought we might perhaps spend these classes in the robotics lab instead?'

The teacher looked as if she might dissolve with relief.

'Yes, yes, I don't mind at all.'

They rushed out.

'You're sure you don't mind missing music?' said Morgana. She definitely wasn't sorry to get away. Being able to play her virtual reality instruments now didn't make her any less tone deaf.

'No, it made me very uncomfortable for Clodagh to be better than me in a subject,' he answered.

Instructor 1107 was in the lab when they arrived. It stood quietly in a corner when not teaching. 'I don't have a class now,' it said. 'And it isn't lunchtime, when you children usually come here.'

They had stayed well clear of the canteen lately,

Jonathan just heading in to grab some food for them before meeting Morgana in the lab.

'We have permission from the music teacher,' said Jonathan.

'I will check this afterwards,' said the robot. 'And I will give you the appropriate punishment if you are lying.'

'Understood,' said Morgana.

'Come on,' said Jonathan, dragging her over to the screens that lined the room. 'I want to show you this code I've been writing for the arm.'

The class were still working on their robotic arms, though, with all the extra attention Morgana and Jonathan had been giving theirs, it was far more dextrous than anyone else's.

'Oh, but I wanted to work on some new fingers,' said Morgana, as Jonathan spilt out lines of code from his scroll on to the screen. 'I was thinking – there's no reason why we need to limit ourselves by following human biology so closely. I think an extra joint in the fingers could make things more interesting. And I wanted to try working with some of the different metals I'd found,' she added, opening her bag to reveal Kitty had even less room than usual, perched on a variety of pieces of scrap.

Jonathan did look intrigued by the idea, but insisted on taking her through his work nonetheless, and Morgana listened as intently as she could while she had all this metal weighing her down, just waiting to be reshaped. She loved the building and creation of these machines, but Jonathan was really impressing on her the importance of understanding everything happening within the circuits as well. 'A body is no good without a brain,' he said time and time again, as she itched to get back to the soldering iron while he explained the significance of all his coding.

However, as always, Morgana was astounded when she saw the results of his work. 'See, it can sense how many fingers I am holding up and just imitates me,' he explained.

'How many fingers am I holding up?' Morgana asked, pushing in front of the arm excitedly, and squealing in delight as it mirrored her three digits.

'There's no point asking, though,' said Jonathan, demonstrating again with a single finger. 'It doesn't have any sound sensors.'

This was generally the time when Morgana asked Jonathan to explain his coding again, now that she was really interested in what it could do, but they were interrupted as the rest of the class joined them from music.

'Ohhhh,' chorused Lisa and Claire, seeming genuinely impressed as they watched the hand move through the numbers Jonathan was holding up.

'Ugh, it's not that good,' said Clodagh, pulling them away.

'They're only putting so much effort in because it's the only way they'll ever have another friend,' said Henry. 'If they build one themselves.'

Morgana and Jonathan looked at each other, and she could tell that he too was already contemplating what this robot friend might be like. They had made such good progress on the arm, surely they could manage the other body parts too? Morgana left school that day feeling giddy again at the potential of everything that surrounded her.

This excitement was much needed to counteract the growing isolation she was sensing back in the woods. She and Esther hadn't spoken since the night of their fight. Morgana knew she was being stubborn, but as time passed and the distance between them grew, she found it even harder to apologize. It was becoming difficult to see how they could ever be friends again.

Turlough was still presenting his hostility as a stand for the magic community, though really Morgana could tell his anger was more hurt that his sister was leaving him behind. Her parents were as kind and loving as they had ever been, but they had no interest in her new life. She had tried to explain some of the new technology that Jonathan was introducing her to, but their faces had grown cold in the glow of her enthusiasm.

'You know this means nothing to us,' said her mother, patting her on the head.

Morgana stayed indoors in a huff as her parents went outside to admire Esther and Turlough's new flying skills. They had moved beyond enchanting objects to carry them from place to place, and could now simply take flight themselves. Morgana felt particularly perturbed as she had been trying to tell her parents about how Jonathan was working on convincing his father to use his influence to expand a teleportation channel out to the woods, allowing her to travel to school in seconds.

'Much more convenient than flying,' she muttered to herself, as everyone outside whooped at the formations Turlough and Esther were tracing in the air, darting between the trees and over their branches into the sky to form great sweeping loops around each other. At one time Esther would have laughed with her at Turlough showing off his skills like this; now she was happy to join him.

Still, the lack of interest from everyone else around Morgana didn't quell her own excitement at the idea of the teleportation to the woods, which she eagerly discussed with Jonathan at the back of their history class the next day.

'It'd be pretty easy to set up,' he explained. 'The complete lack of technology in the mountains means there would be hardly any interference. The only reason it hasn't been done before was that no one wanted to travel from the city to the woods.'

'Or the other way, believe me!'

'Well, someone does now, so I don't see why you should have to get up at the crack of dawn every morning.'

'But even if it's easy enough to do from the technological side of things, it still sounds like a lot of work goes into the set-up. It's hardly going to be done just so one eleven-year-old girl can have a bit of a lie-in in the morning.'

'Well, maybe not usually, but my father might be able to pull a few strings,' said Jonathan, looking suddenly embarrassed at what sounded like a boast. 'I mean, it really wouldn't be a big deal, and technically all communities should be served.'

'And do you really consider a bunch of savages living in trees a community?' asked the slimy voice of Henry. They hadn't noticed he was sitting in front of them.

'Well, I for one would protest any plans. And I'm sure my father would as well,' said Clodagh. 'I can't believe you actually think it's a good idea to give them access to the very teleportation networks they keep interfering with. We need to think of our own safety. Imagine having those violent freaks able to appear amongst us whenever they choose.' She gave a theatrical shiver at the thought.

'You know, if the two of you could come up with something remotely interesting to talk about yourselves, you might not have to resort to listening in on our conversations to give your lives some excitement.'

Both heads quickly snapped round at this admonishment from Jonathan.

'I wish *I* could think of something to say when they're like that,' said Morgana. 'No wonder they think I'm stupid. I turn into a mute whenever they start picking on me.'

'Well, I've had years' more experience of being picked on by that lot. I don't know if it gets easier, but I did realize eventually that how they treat me has nothing to do with anything I do. You could come up with the cleverest comebacks for them and they'd still call you an idiot. It's doubly unfair – but also quite liberating in a way, knowing you might as well be yourself.'

'I suppose,' said Morgana. 'Well, it's easier now

that I have a friend.'

Jonathan smiled sheepishly. 'Anyway, I was thinking we could take this teleportation scheme up with my father in person. My mother asked me to invite you for dinner after school on Friday.'

Morgana's parents were reluctant at first at the thought of her spending even more time down in the city, but they couldn't resist her relentless pleading for long.

'Well, you do seem a lot cheerier now "my friend Jonathan" is mentioned in every sentence,' said her mother. 'And if you insist on leaving the woods, we do want you to be happy beyond them.'

Morgana could hardly wait for Friday to arrive.

Chapter Twelve

It was only on Friday morning that her excitement began to fester into a knot of nervousness in her stomach. She had stopped caring what everyone else at school thought of her – she could do without her nasty classmates and lazy, incompetent teachers, but she was worried about how Jonathan would feel if his parents were disgusted by the wild creature he brought home from the woods. From all she'd heard, they sounded like very important and powerful people. His father was a robotics professor who had become one of the heads of the greatest robot company on the planet. His mother had met his father working in this firm, but was now a lawyer for one of their competitors. They were both deeply ensconced in the world of technology – just the types to take against witches and warlocks.

'You seem very quiet,' said Jonathan, as they left their final lesson. 'You do still want to come for dinner, don't you?'

'Oh yeah, of course!' said Morgana, trying to fashion her nerves into a smile, but not managing much more than a twisted grimace.

'Well, if you're sure,' said Jonathan uncertainly. 'We'd better rush for the teleportation station before the queues start to build up. Better to avoid the lift.'

Morgana felt her excitement begin to grow again as she raced Jonathan up the stairs to where the teleportation station stood. She hadn't even considered how they would be travelling, or she would have figured that Jonathan would naturally go by the most hi-tech means available.

There were only a few people in front of them

when they arrived, panting, at the top of the building. 'You'd better catch your breath before we get in,' said Jonathan. 'They can really take the wind out of you when you're not used to them. Luckily this station can take two people at once. I believe it can be quite a disorientating sensation the first time.'

Morgana's breathing was smoother by the time they were in front of the station, but she could feel her heart pumping as they stepped up on to the platform on which the glass box stood.

The door sealed tightly shut behind them once they entered. Jonathan spoke his address into a small black panel on the wall and there was a blinding flash of white light. Morgana felt an immense pressure pushing in on her from all sides. It was as if she was being compressed into a tiny ball, with such force that she felt she might completely implode. Then, just as suddenly, a stretching sensation swept through her body, and she found herself standing in a similar glass case to the one they had just left behind.

She wasn't standing for long, though, as she

collapsed on her jellified legs. Jonathan didn't seem affected at all as he bounded out, while she pulled herself up the glass walls as best she could and stumbled out after him.

'Well, here we are,' said Jonathan.

As Morgana's eyes began to focus again, the view that surrounded her quickly sharpened her senses. They were standing on what seemed to be one of the tallest buildings on the top level of the city, though it was still dwarfed by the RoboCorp building which overshadowed it. The sun was already low in the sky, and the buildings around them were flickering to life as lights began to illuminate their countless windows. Even at this height there was a dull thrum of traffic from both above and below. The dark mountains in which her home was nestled hemmed in the city almost all the way around. The sea was the other force of nature that checked its growth, though it couldn't be seen – even from this height – through all the concrete and metal.

Morgana could have stayed there all night, transfixed by the view, if a polite cough from

Jonathan hadn't reminded her that his invitation had in fact extended beyond his roof.

'We're on the top floors, so not far to go.'

It was just a short trip down in the lift, and then they were before the thick steel door to Jonathan's home. Jonathan stood squarely in front of it, apparently just waiting. Morgana was about to ask if he had forgotten his key when a face of sorts appeared in the door. Two eyes blinked open above, and what had been a doorknob now looked like a nose that topped off a wide mouth, which stretched apart to speak.

'Good evening, Master Jonathan,' it said, a light shining from its eyes and scanning Jonathan's face before the door swung open before them.

Jonathan's mother was waiting in the hall behind, smiling broadly.

'I heard you coming. Really, that door is one of your father's more ridiculous robots. I'm sure a simple lock would be a lot less trouble. But anyway, at least it let you in. It can be wary of guests, and I wouldn't want anything spoiling your visit, Morgana. You're very welcome to our home.'

'Thanks for having me,' said Morgana, doing her best to remember her manners and not get distracted by all the mechanical creatures she could see moving out of the corner of her eye. Luckily Jonathan's mother was the kind of person who naturally held your gaze. She was very tall and beautiful. Her dark skin was gleaming against a light silver dress cut in a triangular shape, and her hair hung in thick braids down her back.

'Well, I just had to meet you. Jonathan has hardly stopped talking about you. Dinner is almost ready,' she said, taking Morgana's cloak from her. 'So, you can have a look around and I'll let you know when it's done.'

This suited Morgana, as despite her hunger she couldn't wait to see Jonathan's workshop. She knew that was where all her devices had originated, along with many other contraptions that Jonathan had shown her, or described to her if they had been one of the few that ended in combustion.

'Come on,' said Jonathan. 'This way. And you can let Kitty loose now.'

Kitty bounded ahead, always excited at her

evening liberation, but Morgana followed more slowly through the apartment. She kept getting sidetracked by all the objects she wanted to examine, all so mundane to Jonathan that he didn't even think to explain them to her. She wasn't familiar with the materials anything was made from, and nothing seemed to be of a defined shape. She thought Jonathan was about to run right into a table in his excitement to show off his workshop, but it simply shifted its edges to let him pass.

'Is that table alive?'

'No,' said Jonathan, glancing back at it. 'Just self-adjusting. I mean, *we* don't really need it, because we have a big place, but most people's apartments are tiny, so it lets them make the most of their homes. All furniture comes like that these days.'

Morgana didn't like to correct him, but, thinking of the furniture her parents had magicked together from some fallen oaks, she knew that there were still simpler tables around.

The furniture didn't hold Morgana's fascination long. There were too many robots drifting about the place. One was cleaning in the living room, though it had an easier job than the feather duster that was set to work about Morgana's home, as the rooms were sparsely decorated, with none of her cabin's cauldrons and potion bottles and charms. A glimpse in the kitchen showed that while Jonathan's mother might be supervising the dinner, she wasn't doing the cooking herself. One robot was chopping vegetables and popping them into what Morgana thought was its head at first, but then realized was actually a pot of boiling water set atop its shoulders. Another machine was wandering around the kitchen tidying up. Morgana noticed a warm glow coming from its belly, and as it turned to face her, she saw a delicious-looking chicken was roasting inside it while it went about its chores.

'Oh, I am glad we're not having more of the kind of food we get in school,' said Morgana, who hadn't been particularly looking forward to the dinner part of the evening.

'Eugh,' said Jonathan. 'No, thankfully my parents can afford non-lab-grown food. That school stuff is completely nutritious, gives you everything you need, but it's never really satisfying somehow. Hurry up, though – I can introduce you to all the home appliances after dinner. I want to show you my own creations first.'

They carried on to the end of the corridor, where a metal door glided open in front of them. Morgana gasped at the wonders it revealed.

There were a number of workbenches around the room. On these were laid the deconstructed parts of what seemed to be several robots. Here and there were metal arms and legs with wires hanging out. One half-excavated head blinked its single eye forlornly as the electronics that made up its mind spilt out on to the table. Most exciting, though, was the fact that these robots were still being worked on. A pair of rather cumbersome-looking robots stood at one of the tables, adjusting the mechanics that lay before them.

'Wow, Jonathan! Did you really make all this? You have robots advanced enough to work on robotics?'

'Well, I didn't build those from scratch. I simply repurposed them. And to be honest they are quite slow at their work and can only be trusted with the simplest of tasks, but I have learnt a lot from them. And I'm looking at programming some upgrades which will enhance them significantly.' He pulled out his scroll and projected a reading of a great deal of code that Morgana couldn't even begin to understand yet, but she nodded away as he took her through the changes he was making. 'And with all that implemented, I think the robots they help me build will be even more advanced again.'

'Can a robot make another that is better than itself?'

'Oh yeah!' said Jonathan. 'I mean, humans have been capable of creating creatures more advanced than ourselves for almost a century.'

'Really?' said Morgana incredulously. 'I mean, I've seen some incredible machines since I've been coming to the city, but nothing that seems close to a person. They might be better at doing whatever they were designed for, but they're all so, well . . . robot-y.' She couldn't explain exactly what it was that made robots inferior in her eyes, when all that she had learnt about them in her brief studies had shown the immense power and intelligence they were capable of.

'Yes,' said Jonathan, understanding what she meant anyway. 'But that is mostly down to the limits the law places on the science. If the engineers and programmers were permitted to give them free will and emotional intelligence, and widen the range of capabilities of individual machines, then we could be producing machines that would far outstrip any human.'

Jonathan's eyes were shining as he described this super-robot, and Morgana's mind raced as she realized that, despite her supposed love for all things robotic, she had no idea of the true potential of the field.

Before she could ask Jonathan any of the questions welling up inside her, their minds were brought back to reality.

'Dinner's ready!' came a voice, as if from inside the room itself.

'Coming!' Jonathan answered, and they made their way towards the delicious smells wafting from the dining room. There they found their dinner spread across a large glass-topped table with steel legs. The succulent roast chicken was sitting proudly in the centre, surrounded by bowls of vegetables, potatoes and fresh bread. Morgana's mouth was already beginning to water before she spied the piping-hot apple pie waiting on the side-board. Jonathan didn't seem aware of the delicious feast before him – he was just staring at the three place settings.

'Is Dad not coming?'

'I'm afraid there's no sign of him yet,' his mother answered.

'But I reminded him that Morgana was coming over when I saw him on Monday.'

'I know, love, and I reminded him again this morning. You know he's been very busy lately.'

'I know,' said Jonathan with a sigh, sinking into his chair. He kept quiet for the start of the meal, but Morgana had lots to chat about with his mother, who wanted to know all about her life in the woods and how she was finding her new school. Jonathan joined the conversation as Morgana excitedly explained all they had been doing together.

The whole table was quickly silenced again as they heard the front door open and a soft tread coming down the hall. It was heading straight past the dining room when Jonathan called out: 'Dad! Dad, we're in here!'

His father appeared in the doorway. He was a tall, thin man, with a shining bald head, and thick glasses which only accentuated the deep bags under his eyes. He wore sleek but practical-looking overalls, similar to what Jonathan always wore.

'Oh, are you still eating? It looks wonderful, but I really must head downstairs to my workshop. I have a lot more to do before the day is out.' He sounded very preoccupied as he spoke.

'I really think it would be best if you join us,' said Jonathan's mother, a certain steel to her voice that Morgana hadn't noticed before. Jonathan's father came into the room.

'Yes, perhaps you're right,' he said, taking a spare plate from the sideboard and sitting down. 'I should probably get something to eat. I have a long night's work ahead of me.' His eyes fell suddenly on Morgana. 'Oh, hello, I didn't realize we had a guest.'

'Dad,' said Jonathan, his voice strained, 'this is Morgana. I told you she was coming. You said you'd be here.'

'Morgana? Oh yes, the witch girl.'

Morgana felt her cheeks redden. She reached a hand down towards Kitty for reassurance.

'Not that that's a problem,' Jonathan's dad said hurriedly. 'No, no. It's wonderful, wonderful . . . really wonderful.'

They all turned back to their dinners mutely. After a few minutes Jonathan cleared his throat.

'Dad, have you been able to look into setting up a teleportation link to the woods yet?'

'What?' said his father, who had been deep in thought. He sounded as startled as if he had just been teleported into the room himself.

'The teleportation. To the woods.'

'Ah, yes. I mean no. No, I've not had the time, Jonathan. I'm really far too busy at work . . .' He trailed off, drifting back into a reverie.

'Jonathan, tell your father how you're getting on

with your robots in your workshop,' said his mother loudly, bringing her husband's attention back to the table.

'They're coming on really well,' said Jonathan enthusiastically. 'I have two performing basic robotic engineering already, so I think I'm going to be able to create something really impressive. I mean, impressive for my age – nothing like your work. I haven't asked yet, but I'm hoping Morgana will help me with one I've just begun.' He turned to smile at her. 'She really is a natural engineer. I was showing her my workshop before—'

'Very good, very good,' his father interrupted. 'And speaking of workshops, I really must be getting down to mine. Very nice to meet you, Megan.' He pushed away his barely-disturbed plate and dashed out of the room.

'Well, kids, who fancies dessert?' said Jonathan's mother brightly.

No one ever ate apple pie as sombrely as Jonathan ate his.

'So, what about this robot you need my help with?' asked Morgana. 'I'd love to hear more.'

'Really?' said Jonathan, raising his head.

'Of course! It sounds so exciting.'

'Why don't you take Morgana out to the domed gardens?' suggested his mother. 'Get some fresh air.'

'OK,' he said with a weak smile. 'Let's go.'

They left the apartment and got the lift down to a marbled lobby. The park was right next to the building.

'The door's just been fixed,' said Jonathan as he pushed it open to let them into the little oasis of green. 'It was smashed by some vandals.'

'Oh, really? That's terrible,' said Morgana, not looking directly at him. As they took a seat under one of the trees, she clutched Kitty to her chest – with her legs hidden, just in case a robot chicken appeared to reclaim his claw.

'I'm sorry about my father,' said Jonathan quietly.

'You've nothing to apologize for. He seemed a very nice man.'

'He is, he really is. I mean, when he's here. But when he's like he was tonight he might as well be shut away in his workshop. And he's always like that lately. He's been so busy trying to work out what's causing the disruptions in the city's technology. I thought he'd be different with you here, though, and when I told him about my plans for my robots. I thought he might notice me then, but I guess not.'

'Well, I don't think he was really listening, to be honest,' said Morgana, though she quickly realized that this might not be a very positive thing to say. 'And anyway, *telling* him is one thing, but if he actually *saw* everything you're building I'm sure he'd be amazed.'

'You think so? You know, I meant what I said before. I'd love for you to help me on this new robot. I know you still have a lot to learn, but you've such a fresh way of looking at everything that it really does help. You make me consider things from a different perspective. And you have a way with metal that I've never mastered. I think together we can make something that will really get his attention. Get everyone's attention, I mean.'

'I'd be honoured, Jonathan, if you really think I can be of any help. But you promise to let me know if I'm getting in the way?'

'I don't think that will happen, but it's a deal,' he said, looking much cheerier. 'Come on so. I have some initial plans you can have a look at before you leave.'

Chapter Thirteen

Over the next few weeks, the building of this new robot began to consume the lives of Morgana and Jonathan. Every class was spent huddled in the corner discussing plans. The teachers were happy to leave them to it – it meant they no longer had Jonathan showing them up with his brilliance, answering other students' questions when they couldn't, and posing his own questions that left them completely perplexed. They were also glad they didn't have to deal with Morgana any more. None of them could be bothered trying to put in the effort to catch her up with seven lost years of education, so they were more than willing to let Jonathan fill her in.

Nearly every evening and weekend was spent in Jonathan's workshop, tinkering away on the machine. It was slightly taller than them, with a boxy head and square body, though Morgana hoped to take some of the sharpness off its edges later. She also wanted to get more of a shine to its dull grey metal, but they were focused on its functions for now. What she really wanted was to see it walk.

'Come on,' she said, beckoning to it from across the room. 'Just a few steps – come on, Proto!'

'Morgana,' said Jonathan, 'it's not Proto, it's Prototype 201119. Proto sounds like a name.'

'Well, Prototype 201119 sounds like a *bad* name.'

'You know what I mean,' he said. 'It's not allowed.'

'What about Kitty? That's a name and you use it.'

'Well, I don't think the law is as strict for

non-humanoid machines, and we don't know Kitty's properly assigned code. We do know Proto's. I mean Prototype 201119's!'

As they were arguing they missed Proto's first shaky step, but couldn't miss the loud crash as he fell instantly to the floor.

'Oh, Proto!' cried Morgana, rushing forward. Jonathan was too worried about the robot to correct her this time.

Proto was fine, but they never got him beyond one step. No matter how hard they worked, they just couldn't keep pace with their growing ambitions for their machine.

'We need it to be swifter,' said Morgana. 'I want it to be able to move like a human, only it should be even more agile.'

'It's its mind I'm worried about,' said Jonathan. 'If we can't up the amount of data it's able to process, it will never be as smart as we want it.'

'It will be the finest robot the world has ever seen,' said Morgana, getting carried away by their plans.

'Well,' said Jonathan, not sounding so bold, 'I

certainly think it could be the best robot someone of our age has produced. I hope to impress my father, but I don't think we could ever surpass him. We need to be a bit more realistic, Morgana. I'm sure he has stuff in his workshop that we could only dream of.'

'But that's it!' cried Morgana. 'You're right, but why should we only dream of it when we have it right under our feet? Here we are, with the work of one of the greatest robotics minds in the world just downstairs, and we're still studying from this basic school stuff. Think of what we could learn down there.'

'Well, yes,' said Jonathan. 'But just because it's in my house doesn't mean we can just wander in. There could be secret stuff going on down there.'

'Surely anything top secret wouldn't be in his personal workshop.'

'True,' admitted Jonathan. 'Anything classified wouldn't be let beyond RoboCorp, but my dad can be secretive about his own work too.'

'I'm sure he wouldn't mind his own son having a quick look.'

'Well, he's never shown me anything before,' said Jonathan quietly.

'Never?' said Morgana, in shock.

'He's always too busy,' said Jonathan. 'He can't waste any time trying to explain his work to me.'

'If he ever took the time to talk to you, he would realize that you're more than capable of understanding whatever he's got going on down there. Or better still, let's take a look, and when we're able to adapt his work to our own robot, that will definitely show that you understand it.'

A steely look appeared in Jonathan's eyes.

'You're right. I'll never produce anything that will get his attention without at least trying to match his work. So I suppose we can take a quick look. Kitty has to stay here, though, so she doesn't make a mess.'

Jonathan's mother was in her study, but was remotely attending a meeting in Shanghai, and so was completely unaware of her surroundings. Though she was physically present in the apartment, the world she saw around her was an office building thousands of kilometres away. Despite this, Morgana and Jonathan still took the precaution of tiptoeing down the corridor that opened on to the stairs leading down to the professor's workshop. There was a keypad on the door, into which Jonathan entered a code.

'I may have looked over his shoulder before,' said Jonathan sheepishly. 'Not the tightest security, but I suppose he figured that anyone who could get past the security into the apartment was someone he could trust not to invade his personal space.'

He paused briefly at the top of the stairs, clearly wrestling with his conscience, but Morgana simply brushed past.

'Oh, come on! If he was really that worried about keeping the place private it wouldn't be so easy for a pair of eleven-year-olds to break in.'

Jonathan didn't argue but simply ran after her down the stairs. There was no code for the steel door at the bottom, but it did take the strength of both of them to slide it open. Their effort was worth it when they saw what was inside.

The room was five times the size of Jonathan's

workspace, and that was just the first floor they were on. Through the metal grating they were standing on, they could make out another floor beneath, the dim light just bright enough to reveal a large cube-shaped structure covered in a grubby tarpaulin. Compared to the grim and lifeless scene underneath, the top floor was a-buzz with activity.

A dozen robots were diligently carrying out various tasks, appendages moving too fast for Morgana and Jonathan to even guess what these might be. All of them were either too absorbed in their work to notice the intruders, or simply not programmed to pay any heed to anything but the job in front of them. Around the edges of the room, blurred columns of numbers were speeding down the enormous computer screens that completely covered the walls.

'Wow,' said Jonathan breathlessly. 'I didn't think there was anything like this kind of work going on down here. I thought this was just where Dad did his own personal study, but this is a very high level of production. I didn't even know we had this much space, and it must be completely soundproofed. I've never heard any noise. Why here, though? He has access to factories all over the world producing robots. Why does he need to spend all his time at home making them himself?'

'Well, it's all *we* ever do,' said Morgana, eyes shining in the glow of the screens around her, as she gazed about in wonder. 'And think of the kind of robot we could produce if we could harness just a fraction of the power of these machines.'

'But how could we even try to understand all this? It's beyond us, Morgana. Let's go back.'

Morgana was also feeling overwhelmed in the face of all that surrounded them. It was another reminder of how much she still didn't understand about the age in which she lived, but it was also an opportunity for her to learn more than she ever thought possible, and she couldn't turn away.

'Well, we're here now,' she said. 'We might as well have a look around. We can't say for sure that everything is beyond us when we're barely in the door.'

A hush fell over the pair as they gingerly made their way over the metal grids of the floor to where the robots were at work.

'I think they're building a robot,' said Jonathan, eyes racing to keep up with the swiftness of their limbs.

'See? It's not that different from our operations,' said Morgana. 'Probably a simpler robot helping to construct a more complex one as well.'

'Yes, but that simple robot looks about a thousand times more complex than we ever dreamt our creation could be. And how powerful must these programmes be if they need computers like that to run them? There's probably even more amazing equipment downstairs, just sitting doing nothing in the dark.'

Suddenly there was a loud crashing sound from below, as if the equipment had come to life in answer to this accusation of idleness. Morgana recovered from the fright more quickly than Jonathan.

'What *is* down there?' she pondered aloud. 'It does look like it's just been cast aside, whatever it is. Perhaps we could make use of it. Your father would probably never even miss it.'

'I think we should go,' said Jonathan, still sounding uneasy.

Another strange noise only confirmed this instinct in him, but it sent Morgana clattering down the staircase. 'Come on, Jonathan. We have to at least have a peek.'

He followed her reluctantly, as the sounds from beneath seemed to grow with the din of Morgana's descent. It sounded like metal rattling against metal. Then a different sound rang clear over the commotion.

'Help me!'

Morgana and Jonathan stopped, frozen in their stride. It was a soft female voice, melodic but full of fear.

'Was that you, Morgana?' whispered Jonathan.

'You know it wasn't,' she hissed back.

'But who else—?'

'Please help me,' the same voice interrupted. They could tell now that it was coming from the structure in the centre of the room, from whatever was beneath those grimy coverings.

'Only one way to find out,' said Morgana,

striding forward.

'Wait! Morgana, we don't know what could be in there.'

'You mean who,' she said, already grabbing a corner of the material draped over the sides and tearing it down with a determined tug.

A cage stood in the centre of the room. A woman stood calmly inside. She didn't reach out, but stood oddly still, white-blonde hair hanging around her face, her skin almost translucent. Morgana and Jonathan stared, mesmerized for a moment, forgetting everything else, until she spoke in that same voice that had called to them before.

'Please, set me free.'

'But who are you? How did you end up down here?' Jonathan stuttered out.

'I have always been here. I have known nowhere else.'

'What do you mean?' asked Morgana, Jonathan now too shocked to even speak. 'Who are you?'

'I am Ingrid.'

'And why are you in my father's workshop?'

Jonathan said.

'This is where he made me.'

'You're a . . . you're a . . .'

'Robot,' breathed Morgana.

'But . . . but . . .' said Jonathan, still struggling to find words to express whatever was racing through his head.

Morgana gazed up at Ingrid in awe. The more closely she studied her, the more uncanny and less human she seemed. Her paleness was not the pink and white of Morgana's skin but a complete lack of pigmentation. The same was true of her hair and eyes. She was also missing small human flourishes: eyelashes, fingernails. But these were small absences really. She would never suspect this was a machine before her. It was a marvel.

'I've never seen anything like you,' she breathed.

'That's because she shouldn't exist,' Jonathan said. '*It* shouldn't exist. Robots like that are illegal. They're too . . . too . . .'

'Human,' suggested Ingrid. 'And like any human, I don't want to be kept in a cage. Whether I should exist or not, I do, and I want to leave here.

Please let me out.'

There was a crack in her voice, almost as if she might cry. *But surely she can't,* thought Morgana. *Robots don't feel, not in that way.* But if she did, it really was too cruel to leave her in here.

Morgana stepped forward and shook the bars of the cage, as if testing their strength. 'Help me, Jonathan,' she said, but he was already dragging her away.

'We have to get out of here,' he said, flinging the covering back over the cage.

'We can't leave her,' she said, as he pushed her towards the stairs.

'She's – *it's* a machine, Morgana,' he shouted. 'Please, we have to get away. You don't understand what this all means.'

The panic in Jonathan's voice frightened Morgana. Suddenly, she wanted to get away too. She raced with him towards the door. Ingrid's voice echoed as they slammed it shut behind them.

'Please help me.'

They panted breathlessly as they reached the top of the stairs and stumbled out into the corridor. Jonathan's eyes glittered strangely.

'You should go, Morgana.'

'But . . .'

'Please, Morgana, leave.'

She didn't know what to say. She left.

Chapter Fourteen

Jonathan hardly looked at her as she sat down beside him in class the next day.

'Jonathan, we need to talk about what we saw . . .'

'Shhh, not here,' he said, but he made firm eye contact at last. 'Later, I promise.'

Morgana hardly heard a word that was said in those morning classes, and Jonathan seemed pretty unresponsive to what was going on around them as well. They rushed to the empty robotics lab as soon as the bell rang for lunch, without even bothering to dash to the canteen for food.

'OK,' said Morgana, as soon as they were sure that they were completely alone. 'You said I didn't understand. So explain to me.'

'Morgana,' he said. 'You don't know how much trouble my father would get in if people found out what he was doing. The laws around how advanced robots can be made are taken very seriously. It's seen as fundamental to our society. As soon as it was clear how far the science could go, limits were put in place to ensure the future of mankind. My father has ignored these completely.'

'But why? Why has he done this?'

'I've no idea,' shrugged Jonathan. 'Because he could?'

'You mean you didn't ask him? About any of it?'

'No, I couldn't tell him we'd broken into his workshop. And, anyway, I didn't want to talk to him, I didn't want to hear what he had to say.'

'Well, there's only Ingrid then, who can help us make sense of this. I'm not saying we have to set her free, Jonathan – I can understand you're scared for your family, but I think we need to go back down there, hear what she has to say.' She took a breath to launch into all the reasons they needed to talk to this robot again, but Jonathan interrupted.

'I was thinking the same thing. I want to know how this happened. What he was planning. And I guess I want to understand her more. It, I mean.'

'I keep thinking of it as her too,' admitted Morgana. 'The way she looked, the way she spoke to us.'

'I keep picturing her behind those bars,' said Jonathan. 'I do want to set her free. I don't know why, but I do. But then I have a feeling it'll cause a whole world of trouble.'

The most they were willing to risk for now was another visit downstairs at Jonathan's house. 'Mum is working late, and Dad won't be home for hours,' Jonathan explained as they headed straight to the door leading to his father's workshop.

They both took a deep breath as they opened the door. The descent felt much longer to Morgana today. They didn't speak as they made their way past the working robots and down to the lower floor. Morgana noticed Jonathan's hand was trembling slightly as he made to tear down the covering on the cage.

Ingrid was standing calmly in the centre.

'I was hoping you would be back,' said Ingrid. 'I don't suppose it is to release me?'

Morgana didn't know what to say to that.

'I'm sorry,' said Jonathan. 'We want to, but we can't. I don't think you realize what would happen to my dad if people found out.'

'I understand the consequences, as did he when he chose to make me. But I think he only realized fully what he was doing when he saw me completed. I think his own achievement frightened him. That's why he abandoned me down here.' She sounded cold as she spoke, but then her tone softened again suddenly. 'But that is not your fault, children. And I understand your fears for your father.'

Morgana and Jonathan looked at each other helplessly. They didn't know what to say to that. Luckily Ingrid continued speaking. 'Why were you down here in the first place?' she asked.

'Oh, well, we were trying to learn more about robotics,' said Morgana. 'We weren't expecting to find the greatest robot ever or anything.'

'I'm flattered,' said Ingrid, with the first smile Morgana had seen from her. It just added to the weight of guilt she already felt in her stomach. 'So, you are hoping to follow in your father's foot-steps?' she said, turning to Jonathan.

'Yes,' he said instinctively, but then shook his head. 'But no. I mean, yes, I do want to build robots. So does Morgana – but not like my father, not so carelessly.'

Ingrid didn't comment on this assessment of his father's work.

'So, what kind of robot are you working on now?'

They started to explain slowly, feeling awkward explaining their slow progress to this wonder. But she seemed genuinely curious, and they found themselves giving detailed explanations of all the minutiae of their work.

'Oh, I can help with that, no problem,' Ingrid said, as they described the latest hurdle they were facing. 'Just bring it down with you next time.'

'Next time?' said Morgana.

'Well, I do hope you will be back to visit. If I am to be stuck down here, it would be nice to have some intermittent company.'

Talk of a next visit made Jonathan realize that they should probably bring this one to a close. 'Oh no, Mum will be back soon. We have to go.'

The children hurried away, making no promises as Ingrid called out to them.

'I hope to see you soon.'

Chapter Fifteen

Morgana was all ready to return for a visit, but Jonathan wouldn't hear of it. 'It's not safe, Morgana,' he said as they ate their lunch in the robotics lab. 'We just have to try and forget about her now.'

'We'll never make any great progress with our robot without her, though. Think of what we could achieve with her help.'

'Well, maybe we should be a bit less ambitious. Anyway, we're spending so much time on our new robot, you don't think we're neglecting Kitty, do you?' asked Jonathan, trying to grab a hold of the robot cat as she tore across their work bench, sending parts flying. 'She could probably do with some attention too.'

'Well, she seems to be working pretty well to me,' said Morgana, as Kitty shot out of Jonathan's grasp again. He made another lunge for her, then froze midway as the door was flung open.

'Wait a moment, guys. I think I left my bag in here,' Clodagh called out behind herself, not even noticing that the room was occupied. When she did spot them, she looked disgusted, then erupted into laughter.

'What on earth is that . . . thing?'

'Nothing,' said Morgana, blushing deeply as she tried to bundle Kitty back into her bag.

'Oh no, I need to see this,' said Clodagh, rushing forward. Her gang appeared in the doorway, looking gleeful already at the anticipation of some torment.

'Get away from her,' pleaded Morgana as Clodagh grabbed Kitty from behind.

'*Her?*' screeched Claire. 'Aw, so Jonathan isn't

your only friend. Hahaha.'

'Ugh, do you really want to be touching that thing?' asked Henry. 'It's probably rancid if it belongs to her.'

'Ewww! I hadn't thought of that,' said Clodagh, letting go all of a sudden.

Morgana was sent flying backwards as the tension was released and Clodagh was left holding Kitty's tail. Kitty let out a yelp as wires sparked from her bum. Morgana didn't have time to comfort her; she placed her down and rushed to join Jonathan, who was trying to snatch the tail back from the girls as they threw it between themselves over his head.

Morgana's reflexes weren't any better than Jonathan's, though, and they ended up knocking each other over in their attempts to grab it. The girls collapsed into such raucous laughter at this that someone dropped the tail.

'Aha!' said Morgana, holding it aloft triumphantly.

'Well, that's not much use without an ancient lump of scrap metal to attach it to.'

Morgana spun round in horror to see Clodagh holding Kitty by one of her back paws.

For a moment the two girls stood completely still with their eyes locked on each other. It was Clodagh who broke the stare, racing out of the room with Kitty. Morgana tore after her, but wasn't quick enough to catch her before the lift doors slammed closed.

'It's going up,' called Jonathan from behind.

The two of them pelted for the stairs, taking two steps at a time, all the way up to the top of the building where they found Clodagh, standing with one hand on her hip and the other dangling Kitty over the edge.

'Don't!' cried Morgana, anger and terror swirling around inside her.

Clodagh smirked back at her.

'Going to try some of your magic on me again?'

Morgana glared at her. She had never before tried to summon magic so wilfully, but she didn't know what to do beyond pleading with herself to do something. She wished she had paid more attention in her magic lessons. She felt nothing.

Jonathan's warning was pointless.

'They're filming you, Morgana. Don't let her catch you out.'

As Morgana turned her head towards Jonathan, she saw that Lisa and Claire had arrived, scrolls out to capture any illegal magic that she might perform. Anyway, Morgana knew that even if she could summon anything like the power she had released in the canteen, there was no way she could control it enough to get Kitty back.

Clodagh seemed to realize that Morgana wasn't going to rise to her challenge, so she tried a different tack.

'What would you give to keep this piece of junk together?'

'Anything! Please, Clodagh, give her back.'

'Maybe . . .' said Clodagh, gently swinging Kitty back and forth as she pawed at the air, meowing frantically. 'If you promise me one thing.'

'I promise! I promise!'

'Well, that doesn't count. You don't even know what I want you to do yet.'

'Just tell us what you want,' demanded Jonathan.

'I want her to promise to never show her face in this school again.'

'You can't be serious,' said Jonathan.

Clodagh let Kitty slip a little further through her fingers in answer. Morgana started forward, her arms outstretched.

'OK, OK! I promise.'

Clodagh fixed her with a cold stare.

'Say it!'

'I swear,' said Morgana. 'I swear to leave this school and never come back.'

Kitty clattered to the ground as Clodagh threw her at Morgana's feet. Morgana snatched her up, tears of relief spilling down her cheeks.

'Well, what are you waiting for?' snarled Clodagh. 'Get out!'

Morgana rose to her feet and rushed for the stairs.

'Wait!' called Jonathan, chasing after her. 'You can't just let her win like that. You belong here as much as any of them!'

'But I don't feel like I belong. I sometimes think I never should have come. It was crazy to think I could find a place for myself here.'

'You have, though,' said Jonathan, racing ahead to slow her march down the stairs and towards the main entrance. 'Doesn't our friendship count for anything?'

'Of course it does, Jonathan. But it just makes life difficult for you as well.'

'I don't care. Morgana, please don't go.'

She paused before the door to turn to him, her heart breaking at the hurt in his voice.

'I really don't want to. I feel I could be happy here if they would just let me. But none of that matters now. I swore I would leave.'

'So what?' said Jonathan. 'It's just words. Who cares if you break a promise to someone like Clodagh?'

'I do,' said Morgana. 'I don't know much about magic, but swearing is a kind of magic, one of the most ancient kinds. Words like that truly bind, and it's dangerous to break them.'

'What are you still doing here?' called Clodagh from the top of the stairs. 'Too stupid to find your way out?'

Morgana was out of the door with just a quick glance back at Jonathan.

'I'm so sorry.'

She didn't give him a chance to reply, too afraid she might not be forgiven.

Chapter Sixteen

The next morning Morgana left her home at the usual hour. She wasn't sure why she didn't just tell her parents that she wasn't going back to school. They probably would have been delighted, but it would have felt so final to admit that her school days were over, so she simply wandered aimlessly into the city.

She thought it would bring her some relief to spend time in the place she loved, but somehow it only deepened her sadness. She felt even further removed from everything that surrounded her.

Every robot was a mystery she would never solve, every train that zipped overhead was one she would never have reason to take, every dirty look thrown at her she would never prove wrong. And Kitty was still skittish from her ordeal the previous day, almost tripping Morgana up as she wound nervously between her legs, not wanting to be apart from her.

Morgana's despair became so overwhelming that she had to escape, and to somewhere she had never thought she would turn for comfort – the Undercity. Perhaps *this* was where she belonged: not quite part of the mountains, not quite part of the city. She ambled through the winding streets and alleyways, trying to picture a place for herself, but no one here seemed to fit. For the first time she felt some sympathy for the Undercity's inhabitants. They, like her, were struggling against a world that didn't want to make room for them.

Morgana headed home as the usual school closing time approached. The next day she kept to the woods, heading deep into the trees, as far from the village as she dared to stray without having to worry about finding her way back. She was still miserable, but Kitty seemed happier at least, and Morgana couldn't resist her infectious energy. She found some distraction from her thoughts as they raced by the river and clambered up trees.

'How did you get so mucky being in the city all day?' asked her mother suspiciously when she arrived home, having skirted around the village so she could appear from her usual path.

'Oh . . . well, I tripped just before I got to the village,' Morgana answered, trying to brush some of the dirt off Kitty.

'Well, be more careful tomorrow. I can't send you down to the city in clothes like that. They already think we're uncivilized.'

So on the following days Morgana couldn't even enjoy the freedom of the woods, no matter how much Kitty pestered her to join in with her gambolling. The days stretched out endlessly. Eventually Morgana turned to her scroll for some distraction, though she hadn't been able to face it since leaving school. The tears stung her eyes as Jonathan's messages began to flash up.

Where are you?
Please come back.
You can't let Clodagh keep you away.
We can still be friends.

She knew he really meant that last one, but she didn't see how it could work. Their lives would just be so different from now on. She realized she was going to have to accept it and try to carve some place for herself in the magic community. She couldn't cower away in the forest for ever.

She turned and followed the river back towards the village. As she reached it, she could hear the clatter and laughter of lunch. She peeped through a gap in the houses and saw that the communal table occasionally used for dinner had been brought out for the meal, and everyone was gathered around passing great heaped plates between each other.

'We don't get to do this enough,' said Ms Garcia. 'So good to have the opportunity to have everyone sit down together to eat.'

'Well, almost everyone,' said Morgana's mother.

'Everyone who matters,' retorted Mr Roche

with a stern look. 'Don't think there isn't a reason that we decided to take our village meal during the day this time, when everyone within the village is someone who truly belongs here, who wishes to be part of the community.'

Morgana saw her parents stare into their plates, and she could almost feel Turlough's fury from where she stood, and she knew she would certainly feel the brunt of it later. If she hadn't already changed her mind about making an appearance, the thought of facing Turlough at the peak of his anger would have convinced her. She turned again towards the trees and headed back into the lonely shelter they offered her. She felt that if she had anywhere else to go in the world, she might never return to the village where she was so unwanted by everyone but her family. Especially when her presence just caused them pain and embarrassment.

But then a loud scream cut through the air to reach her, and she was instantaneously racing back to the home she had been thinking of abandoning just moments before.

As she reached the village clearing, she spotted

some familiar uniforms stamping through the flee-ing figures that had dispersed from the table.

'Where is she?' one of them barked. 'Don't worry, this isn't a regular inspection. No need to hide your other brats. We're just looking for that one troublemaker.'

Morgana was crouching behind one of the houses. As she peered around the corner, she saw her father step forward.

'I believe it's my daughter you are talking about. She's at school.'

'That's just the problem,' said the inspector, knocking a chair over as he approached her father. 'She isn't. Hasn't been for over a week.'

Her father's brow clouded over.

'Then where could she be?' her mother asked no one in particular as she clutched at her cloak.

'Ha, like you don't know,' laughed one of the other inspectors.

'We really don't,' said her father, fighting to maintain his composure. 'She's been leaving for school every morning and returning home at her usual time.'

'Perhaps,' said the head inspector. 'But you can hardly expect us to simply take the word of a warlock. Tear the place apart, boys.'

'I'm here, I'm here!' cried Morgana, leaping out before they had a chance to touch anything.

'Morgana!' Her mother tried to rush towards her, before being grabbed from behind.

Morgana's father stood frozen for a second, torn between helping his wife and protecting his child. The inspectors took advantage of his confusion, two of them grabbing him by the arms while the head inspector stood barely a centimetre from his face.

'See, can never trust any of you magic filth.'

'He didn't know. None of them knew. I was hiding,' said Morgana, trying to pull the inspector away from her father. The inspector was happy to turn his attentions to her instead, pulling her up by the scruff of her neck until they were almost eye to eye.

'I warned you,' he snarled, flecks of spit hitting her face. 'I told you I didn't want to be sent chasing up these stinking mountains after you.'

'Then blame me. It was all down to me. My father didn't know anything about it. No one else did.'

'Oh, I do blame you,' he said, flinging her to the ground, and kicking Kitty as she clawed at him with her chicken foot. 'But I'm still taking him away.'

'No,' gasped Morgana as the three of them marched her father forward. She could see her mother holding back a flailing Turlough as she jumped to her feet.

'Don't fight,' said her father sharply as he passed her. 'It won't help. I'll be back soon, Morgana.'

She stared helplessly as they guided him out of the village and down the mountainside.

'Come away, Morgana,' said her mother, putting her arm around her, and pulling her towards their home, past the furious looks and mutinous whispers of their neighbours. 'Turlough, inside!'

Turlough barged in after them, but didn't get a chance to unleash his rage on Morgana. His mother stepped between them before he even opened his mouth.

'Morgana does not need you to make her feel bad about what has happened. You know as well as I that your sister would never wish any harm to come to your father. We all need to support each other now and be here waiting for him when he returns, which he will.'

Morgana would have found it easier just to listen to whatever tirade Turlough had planned. She could have brewed some anger to match his own, but now they just had to feel the full weight of their despair. Turlough turned in silence towards the fire, where he sat brooding till the next morning. Morgana dissolved into hysterical tears, and must have eventually cried herself to sleep, as she woke to the sound of their front door creaking open.

For a second the sadness of the previous night resurfaced, but then she recognized the unmistakeable silhouette in the doorway.

'Dad!'

Turlough already had his arms flung around their father's waist, so Morgana grabbed his leg on the other side. Their exhausted-looking mother leant over the pair of them for a kiss. Eventually he was released from their grip and allowed to take a seat.

'I was just given a warning,' he said wearily. 'They had no grounds to keep me, but they held me in their cells for as long as possible. They will be back for me again, though, if you continue to miss school. Now, I won't force you to go, Morgana, but I need to know what you plan to do, so I can be prepared. We can't have any more secrets.'

'I know,' she said. 'And I made up my mind that I would go back last night, and I do want to, it's just ...'

And then the whole story of Clodagh came spilling out: all the torments and teasing, all the hurt she had been hiding from her family for months.

'We were surprised you seemed to be having such an easy time of it. This is one of the reasons we were afraid to have you in that cruel city.'

'It had been getting better, though, with Jonathan. It was just when they hurt Kitty,' she said, leaning down to give her a pat. 'It's so scary to see your familiar so vulnerable. But Kitty isn't the only one I have to protect.'

'I can protect myself, Morgana,' said her father.

'I know, Dad,' she said. 'You're so brave, but I am too. I'll be back to face them tomorrow. And I'll just have to accept whatever comes from breaking my word.'

'A promise given under duress isn't a real promise, Morgana. You won't be breaking your word,' said her mother.

Turlough, who had been uncharacteristically silent throughout her tale, got up and stormed out of the cabin. But Morgana didn't have time to worry about him being disgusted with her. She needed to steel herself for all that she had ahead of her the next day.

Chapter Seventeen

By the next morning Morgana was no longer worried about what she could expect from Clodagh and her gang. She was just afraid of what she might face from Jonathan. She knew Clodagh must have something particularly terrible planned if she was ever to make an appearance again – she just wished she knew exactly what form this torment might take. With Jonathan, though, she had no idea how he would greet her return, and so many of the possibilities, from anger to indifference, would be devastating.

Her thoughts of Jonathan were pushed from her mind by survival instincts on her arrival at school as Clodagh was almost the first thing she saw as she walked in through the gate. She braced herself for whatever was to come. She saw Lisa and Claire tug at Clodagh's voluminous sleeves and point towards her excitedly. Clodagh didn't do anything but glance her way briefly, then snap at Lisa and Claire, who looked away quickly. Morgana let herself feel some cautious relief. Perhaps they had gone back to their tactic of ignoring her completely, which she could easily live with.

Remaining on guard, she walked by them slowly, holding her breath, but still they made no move, and Morgana exhaled deeply as she entered the building. She didn't quicken her pace as she made her way to class, though, still dreading what reception she might expect there. As she entered the room, she saw that Jonathan was still sitting at the desk they had shared, and she couldn't help taking some hope from this, though it was impossible to read anything but shock in his facial expression as he gazed up at her.

This softened into a smile as she made her way towards him, and he moved up to give her space beside him.

'I'm so sorry,' she said before he even opened his mouth, sitting down heavily in the seat beside him. 'I just couldn't come back after what happened. I was afraid,' she admitted quietly. 'And I know I shouldn't have ignored your messages. I thought it would make it easier to stay away, but it didn't. And I realized everything you had said was right. I can't let people like that take my dreams away from me.'

'I understand,' said Jonathan wisely. 'Well, I didn't at first. I was really mad and sad about everything, but I calmed down, and talked about it with my mum, and realized that it wasn't really about me. And I was sure you'd come back, and you did! How's Kitty?'

'She was pretty shaken up,' said Morgana, opening her bag so he could give her a welcome-back ear scratch. 'So, we're friends again?'

'We never stopped being friends. We have lost a lot of building time on the robot, though, but I managed to make some progress that I can't wait to share with you. Want to come over to mine after school?'

Morgana jogged up to the roof as soon as the bell rang for the end of day, and she and Jonathan were almost the first into the teleportation station. Morgana thought herself a confident teleporter by now, but the sensation of this journey was slightly different, and it was taking longer than usual. She thought she might have been imagining it – it had been a while since she had teleported, after all – but it was soon clear that something had gone seriously wrong when she came tumbling out of a station in some unfamiliar part of the city, with Jonathan nowhere to be seen.

Her head was fogged, and her blood was battering against her veins as if trying to escape from their confines. When her body calmed down enough to allow her to examine her surroundings, it was clear that they were not in the fancy area where Jonathan's building stood. She was probably somewhere on the first level above the Undercity, she realized. But where was Jonathan?

Hands trembling, she searched in her satchel for her scroll to message him, but as she unfurled it, its bright light seemed dimmed and it simply flashed a message at her: *no network available*. If there was a way to fix this herself, Jonathan hadn't shown her what it was. Then she heard footsteps.

'Jonathan?' she shouted, before realizing that there were more steps coming towards her than Jonathan's two feet could account for. It was getting dark already, and none of the buildings around her were giving off any light. She tried to press deeper into the shadows. Then she noticed a metallic twang to the echo of the approaching steps, and felt some of the tension drop away from her body. It was only some robots. She stepped forward again to continue her search for Jonathan.

However, the second she emerged the robots' heads swivelled towards her in unison. Her muscles seized up as they turned fully towards her and stamped forward. Morgana had often been awed by the power of the robots she had encountered, but she had never feared them like she did the three now looming towards her. One was tall and boxy, in direct contrast to the rotund creature at eye level with Morgana. The third in the middle was the closest to resembling a man – though she could tell even in the fading light that he was made from a brilliant copper – but it was this one that gave her the greatest sense of unease, and her feelings were justified.

'We must capture the human.'

Morgana could see no means of escape as they hemmed her in on all sides.

'Stay back,' she cried out, only a slight crack in her voice revealing how panicked she was. She didn't really think she could intimidate these machines, but she tried to glare them down all the same, sizing up exactly which models they were and the material they were made of. Still they continued to step towards her.

'Seize the human,' the most malicious-looking one said.

'You will not,' she said, instinctively raising her hands in what she thought was a futile gesture of protection.

She was not expecting the power that came shooting down her arms and bursting forth through her palms.

Clearly the robots weren't, either, as it knocked them off their feet and sent them flying across the alleyway. They were almost instantly clambering back up again, though, and struggling forward against the force still pulsating from Morgana's hands.

Morgana didn't know how much longer she could keep them at bay. She felt this power was draining her own energy as it poured out of her. Two of the robots didn't seem able to resist it, but the copper fellow had a strange feel to him – she just didn't have the same control over him as she had over the others. He was inching his way forward, and as she tried to concentrate all her force on him, the other two made some progress.

She could see the internal wiring of the middle one's head by the time she noticed some other figures behind them. Her initial reaction was panic – she wouldn't be able to handle any additions to this gang – but then, just as she felt her powers fail her completely, she recognized Jonathan doing his best to get close to the smallest of the robots.

'Jonathan!' she exclaimed in shock, as he managed a firm slap on the side of the small robot's head. As he pulled away she saw that he had left a small metal device attached to its head. She heard some similar noises from the other machines, and turned to see Jonathan's parents administering blows to the other pair of robots. With a loud whirring noise, the trio of machines slumped into lifelessness.

Morgana almost mirrored them as she finally let her hands drop, but Jonathan rushed to her side to give her support.

'Are you all right?' she heard him asking, as though from a distance.

She nodded her head. 'I am, thanks to you,' she said. 'And your parents. But how did you find me?'

'Well, the teleportation network dumped me out not far from here. I managed to boost my signal enough to send out a distress call to my parents.

Your scroll used to be mine, so I was able to trace it using some software I'd installed in case I ever lost it. By the time my parents found me, I could find you.'

'I'm glad you did,' she breathed, feeling some strength come back to her body. 'And that you had those devices you used on them. What were they?'

'Dad had them,' said Jonathan.

'You may have heard the rumour about technological issues we've been facing in the city,' explained the professor. 'You have experienced a teleportation breakdown. There has also been trouble with some of the robots lately, and unfortunately you encountered some of these too. These deactivators have proved the most effective way of dealing with the more aggressive ones – they disable their circuits temporarily. Everyone in work thinks I'm being overcautious, but I have them producing thousands, they're all piled in my office. Don't worry, I'll be able to fix the robots afterwards. I'd prefer if you kept all this to yourself, though. We don't want people to panic.'

'I definitely won't be telling anyone,' said

Morgana. 'Not when it'll be me and the rest of the witches and warlocks that get the blame. You don't think it could be down to me, do you? I mean, if things are getting bad since I arrived and started to use technology, maybe whatever drops of magic I have are interfering and—'

Before she could finish, Jonathan's father had grasped her by the shoulders and pulled her round to face him. 'If there's one thing I'm sure of, Morgana, it's that none of this is your fault,' he said, eyes wide and slightly manic. Morgana was almost frightened of him until he finished, so sadly, 'No, it's not your fault.'

'Sorry Dad was so intense there,' whispered Jonathan, as they all climbed into their shiny red air car, which had been parked a few alleys over. 'He's under a lot of pressure in work with all these incidents.'

'Uh-huh,' said Morgana absent-mindedly, as the doors of the vehicle shut themselves behind them and Jonathan's mother handed her a parachute. She tried not to look too excited as they lifted off the ground. No one seemed to realize this was her first time in one of these flying machines.

'Home!' Jonathan's mother commanded the car, and all danger and distress was quickly forgotten by Morgana as they took off into the sky.

Chapter Eighteen

'You'll have to eat something, Morgana,' said Jonathan's mother, back at their apartment. She ushered them into the dining room, where dinner was waiting. 'I can't send you home hungry. What are your parents going to think of us after all this?'

Morgana stuffed her face full of stew so she didn't have to answer this, knowing that her parents didn't think much of anyone beyond the woods, whether they fed their children or not. And she certainly wouldn't be telling them about the malfunctioning robots. She couldn't quite believe how much time they let her spend in the city now. She wasn't going to risk being banned from Jonathan's place altogether. It was hard enough already, seeing the progress he had made in the time she had been away.

'Proto! Wow! Oh, could you not have waited for me?' she asked plaintively, finding the robot strutting awkwardly across the floor of the workshop. She was too impressed to be really upset, though.

'When I figured out how to do it, I just couldn't wait! But it's not perfect. I couldn't get its leg quite straight.'

'Well, I'm back now. Get the tools out.'

'You are your own tool, Morgana! I saw your power over those robots earlier. You can't deny your magic now, surely.'

'Well, it may be there, but that doesn't mean that I can control it.' She frowned. 'And magic isn't supposed to work on metal. It isn't one of the elements.'

'I don't know much about magic, but maybe

yours is different. Have you tried working with metal before?'

'I think so,' said Morgana. 'But there's no point – magic never comes when I try to call it.'

'That doesn't mean it never will. Have a go.'

She turned to Proto. Jonathan's confidence was infectious. Maybe it *was* possible for her to command these powers herself. She reached her hand over Proto's leg. She thought she could still feel some currents of energy flowing through her from the alley. Perhaps she could do this . . . she wouldn't need as much power to get Proto's leg right, it just required a slight adjustment . . .

As she pictured in her mind what needed to be done, a tingling sensation started up in her arms. 'Something's happening,' she whispered. She redoubled her efforts, focusing harder as she screwed her eyes shut. 'Has it worked?' she asked, under her breath.

'Well,' he said, sounding flustered. 'Not exactly.'

Morgana opened her eyes. The leg was completely unchanged. She blew out her breath in frustration. '*Nothing* happened?'

'Oh, well. It doesn't matter. I'm sure you'll be back anyway, and we can work on it together in the normal way.'

Something about Jonathan's tone rang uneasily with Morgana. She was silent for a moment before she answered. 'I'm sorry if I was coming over too much. I understand if you want to work on this alone. Look how much you've got done without me. I'm obviously getting in the way.'

'No, Morgana, I didn't mean that. I always like having you here, and I work much better with you here too. It's just – well, I was wondering why you've never invited me to your home. Don't you want your family to meet me?'

The honest answer was no, but Morgana felt sure this wasn't the right answer. 'Of course I'd like you to meet my family, but my home is so out of the way.'

'Well, that was something I wanted to tell you! My father sent a message from the office earlier to say that he's arranged the teleportation link to the woods to be set up this week. So it'll be no trouble at all.'

This scuppered Morgana's first excuse.

'But when we're up there we won't be able to work on the robot. The equipment I use to work on Kitty won't be of any use for this.'

'We can take a break for one night. And I thought I could bring Proto, I mean, Prototype 201119 with me. Your family must be curious to see what we've been working on.'

Morgana laughed inwardly at this. She had stopped trying to tell her family anything about her new life, especially if it was robot-related. She could always feel her excitement fade when it came up against their complete disinterest. The only other excuse she had for Jonathan was that she was sure he would be about as welcome in the woods as her robot talk, but she couldn't say this to him. She still remembered her fear that *his* parents wouldn't approve of *her*.

'Well, I suppose . . .'

'Great! Ask your parents when it'd be convenient. I can come over any time.'

Morgana didn't ask her parents that evening. When she came home she found the whole village gathered around the campfire, heated discussions being fanned by the flames.

'Here she is,' shrieked one of the neighbours as she spotted Morgana in the clearing. 'This is all down to that little nuisance, no doubt.'

'Now, now,' said the slow deep voice of her father, the same he used when trying to calm rows between Morgana and Turlough. 'We don't know that this has anything to do with Morgana.' His eyes were accusatory, though, even as he tried to shelter her from blame.

'I . . . I . . . I don't even know what's happened,' stuttered Morgana as glaring eyes flickered at her furiously in the firelight.

'Some men arrived today,' said Mr Roche. He sounded calm, but Morgana recognized that this unnatural stillness in him was a sign of anger. 'Men from below. They put a strange glass box up over there.'

'It has a very peculiar energy,' said her mother. 'We daren't go near it.'

Morgana felt a tremor of guilt knowing that this time she really was the cause of the trouble, but this was overwhelmed by a great thrill at the thought of an actual teleportation station here in the woods.

'Oh,' she said as casually as she could, avoiding Mr Roche's icy gaze. 'Sounds like a teleportation station.'

'Well, it must be down to you, then,' said Turlough, stepping forward. 'Only such a pathetic witch would need a device like that – not that you deserve the name *witch*. I don't know what you get up to beyond these woods, but how dare you bring this danger to our homes? You saw how those men treated Dad. And now they can appear among us whenever they choose.'

More angry muttering erupted at the thought of this new threat, but while Morgana might have felt cowed before the crowd, she had no problem standing up to her big brother.

'I didn't bring it here. The teleportation workers did. And you are seriously overestimating my influence if you think I decide where these things are placed. All communities should be served by the network. None of you have to use it if you don't want to, but I am looking forward to my lie-in in the morning.' She marched into the cabin, shutting the door so forcefully she almost snapped Kitty in two.

'She's just a child,' she heard Esther's mother say.

'But the danger she poses to us and our way of life is beyond her years,' countered Mr Roche.

Morgana fell asleep to the continued sounds of angry discussion around the fire. Waking to a still-frosty atmosphere the next day, she decided that this was as good a time as any to tell them that Jonathan was coming for a visit. There was barely a reaction.

'Very well,' said her father, glancing furtively at the clock. Morgana suddenly understood the tension that still lingered in the air. It was an hour after she usually left for school, so it was clear that she really did intend to use the teleportation machine. In truth, she couldn't wait.

It was her first time teleporting on her own, but she had gone to Jonathan's so often now that she was quite comfortable with it, even if she was a little shaken from the night before. She delighted when she managed to stay upright as she arrived on the roof of the school. She strode past Clodagh and her gawping gang, who were clearly not happy to see that the rumoured teleportation link to the woods had come to pass.

Jonathan was already working on some code for their robot when she reached the classroom.

'My parents said that you can come over tomorrow. They can't wait to meet you.'

She immediately wished she hadn't added that little lie as he grinned up at her. Perhaps it would have been kinder to give him some warning of the type of reception he could expect.

Chapter Nineteen

Jonathan and Morgana burst forth from the teleportation station the next day, the box containing their robot held between them. Morgana's heart lifted a bit as they approached her cabin and she noticed some small signs that preparations had been made for their guest. Not that Jonathan noticed the scrubbed walls – he was too busy staring in fascination at the trees.

'It's so strange seeing so much . . . nature. Makes you realize how unnatural the dome parks really are. Everything just *belongs* here.'

'Here's my house,' said Morgana.

Jonathan looked at it with the same wonder he regarded the trees. 'It's brilliant. It looks right at home here too.'

Morgana could tell this was meant as a compliment, but she didn't know how to respond. She never considered something belonging to the woods in such a positive way. She said nothing, but pushed the door open gently, still wary of what might be to come.

Her parents were sitting stiffly at the table. Clearly they had been in wait for some time. Her mother jumped to her feet at the sight of them.

'Hello, Jonathan. You are very welcome to our home,' she said in a burst of words.

'Thank you,' said Jonathan in a slightly dazed voice, his eyes following the scrubbing brush still working away on its own before widening in amazement as he spotted the knitting needles clicking away unsupported in the corner. Her father's hulking presence brought his attention back to the table.

'Pleased to meet you,' he said, getting up to

shake Jonathan's hand rather formally.

They all stood around in awkward silence until some pans flew through the open door. Morgana could feel the heat of the campfire still emanating from them as they rushed past her face.

'Ah, here's dinner,' said her mother, clearly relieved by the distraction. 'Sit, children, let's eat.'

The conversation began to flow over the food, mostly driven by Jonathan's curiosity. What were those trees? How did they build their house? What spells could they do? How did magic work? There was even a hint of a smile just about visible through Morgana's father's beard as he tried to answer as best he could questions that only the wisest and most powerful of magic folk had any real understanding of.

'It's fascinating,' said Jonathan. 'Nothing I know should make any sense in the face of magic. It contradicts almost everything my world is based on, and yet here you are!'

'Most of your world finds it hard to deal with our existence for that very reason,' said her mother. 'Easier to laugh at us than try to understand us, and perhaps have to question your whole way of life.'

Jonathan nodded, but Morgana couldn't keep quiet.

'I think most people aren't interested in magic because they find us ridiculous.'

'That is the line most of them use,' said her mother sharply.

'I don't know, Morgana,' said Jonathan. '*Why* do they ban magic from the city? I know everyone laughs at magic now, but I think deep down people are still in awe of your powers.'

'Not *her* powers, surely,' laughed a voice from the doorway.

Morgana turned to see her brother had arrived, a look of disgust on his face as he surveyed the scene before him.

'I don't think anyone could be impressed by *her* powers, unless the ability to create a few sparks now and then is a thing of wonder. Now, *my* powers, they are truly something to behold.' Turlough had his eyes locked on Jonathan as he spoke, moving slowly across the room, and he now leered down on him menacingly. Jonathan gulped.

'Jonathan is our guest,' said Morgana's mother. 'If you're going to be unfriendly, Turlough, you should leave now.'

'Yes, come on, Turlough.' Esther was standing by the door, Morgana suddenly realized. 'I think you're overestimating your powers. I'm still flying literal rings around you, and if you want me to help you practise, we'll have to go now, while there's still light.'

Morgana gave Esther a smile, glad that despite the coldness between them she was trying to keep Turlough in check. Esther didn't look at her.

'I'm not going anywhere,' said Turlough. 'I think there should be someone with some sense here while this outsider is in the house.'

He pulled up a chair and sat heavily at the table. Esther joined them, sitting down with a sigh. The food on the table lay forgotten. Esther turned to Jonathan.

'Hello. I'm Esther,' she said, holding out her hand.

'Jonathan,' he mumbled, taking the proffered

hand, still looking flustered under Turlough's intense stare.

'I'm surprised a witch of your talent would bother talking with such an inferior,' said Turlough snidely.

'Turlough,' bellowed his father, rising to his feet.

Esther rolled her eyes in such a way that Morgana knew that she had a scathing reply for Turlough, but she felt she was the one who should stick up for her friend.

'Inferior?! Jonathan has talents you will never understand. He has knowledge far beyond what you can learn in these woods. You couldn't even comprehend half of what he knows.'

Jonathan simply sat there dumbfounded. He wasn't about to proclaim the power of his quiet intellect in the face of the tangible strength of Turlough, who was almost pulsating with rage.

'I don't want any of the knowledge he has. You see, unlike you, my magic isn't so terrible that I need to go chasing lesser wisdom. And you probably don't even have any power over their technology either. They won't share their secrets with one of us. You have nothing.'

Jonathan finally found his voice.

'That is not true,' he said, quietly but firmly. 'Morgana has quickly grasped the basics of computer programming and robotic engineering. And she is building on this every day. Her passion and quizzical mind have been invaluable in building our robot . . .'

'Ha! You're building a robot?' laughed Turlough. 'I suppose it's as impressive as this useless lump,' he said, kicking his foot towards Kitty, who stepped out of the way lightly. She was used to this kind of treatment by now. 'I can only imagine what the two of you would come up with.'

'Well, actually, we brought it with us,' said Jonathan brightly, suddenly oblivious to Turlough's unfriendliness in his eagerness to share their work. He jumped from the table, dived into the box that held their creation, and began assembling the parts, talking excitedly the whole time. 'We've only been working on it for a couple of months. I'd completed a lot of the groundwork before then, but there's only so much you can do on your own, and Morgana rebuilt much of the physical machine. It's quite a simple model now, but we have big plans for it – who knows what it could become?'

He was screwing on the head as he spoke. Morgana felt pride bubbling as she watched Proto come together, but she was irritated too, knowing that her family wouldn't appreciate what they had accomplished. She knew they would just see a poor metallic excuse for a man.

'Watch this,' said Jonathan, turning on the switch.

A humming noise rose from the machine as it came to life.

'Hello, how may I serve you?' it said in a stilted voice.

'Please will you move to the other side of the room?' asked Jonathan.

Obligingly, it paced slowly across the floor, then paused and turned, waiting for more instructions.

'Ha, is that it?' asked Turlough. 'Wow, so you can get a pile of junk from one side of the kitchen to the other.' He waved his hands, and up shot various household objects, which he summoned into the centre of the room. Here they shaped themselves into a crude human form. A broomstick made up the body, from which swung a pair of arms that were usually a spatula and a wooden spoon, and the head was a tin bucket.

'Watch me!' Turlough's voice echoed from the bucket skull, though his lips didn't move. The broom man slid across the floor and circled around the robot.

'Now, how long have you fools spent putting together what took me mere moments?'

Jonathan had been mesmerized by Turlough's broom man, but this question brought him back to his senses.

'Well, while I admit I don't have any real understanding of the magic process, I don't think it's a fair comparison. While we have only been able to get the robot to complete simple tasks, there is a huge amount of brain activity we have to emulate to get to this level. I mean, you projected your voice, but our robot is able to produce simple speech patterns and understand language.'

'Whatever,' said Turlough, refusing to be impressed. Rather than try and get a better understanding of why he should be, he got up to leave. 'I've seen enough.'

Proto had something to say to him, though.

'I'm glad you are leaving. You are very rude.'

The whole room stared in astonishment.

'What did you say to me?' said a furious Turlough.

'I said you were very rude,' Proto answered calmly, in his metallic monotone voice. 'You should treat people with more respect. I include myself in that.'

'I should respect you?' said Turlough, with a slightly nervous laugh. 'Do you let these *things* tell you what to do, Morgana?'

Morgana was too dumbfounded to answer, but her brother was already out of the door anyway.

'It really is amazing,' said Esther to Jonathan, before following Turlough out.

'It is!' Morgana said. More than she even realized. What kind of programmes had Jonathan installed since she last saw Proto?

Jonathan cleared his throat awkwardly.

'You know, you've spent so much time in my workshop, but I haven't seen yours yet.'

'Well, none of us have seen that either,' said her mother. 'But it will probably be more interesting to you, Jonathan. Now I have to make sure you get something proper to eat. Finish off your dinner first and Morgana will show you her . . . stuff,' she finished, waving her hands over the dinner growing cold on the table until it was piping hot again.

They both wolfed down their dinner. Morgana could tell Jonathan needed to speak to her. They rushed to the den with Proto between them. Jonathan was momentarily distracted as he entered.

'Wow!'

Morgana would have liked to think it was her heaps of mangled metal that so impressed him, but Jonathan went straight over to peer at the cauldron of something purple and bubbling that Esther was brewing, and inspect the jars of finished potions she had lining the walls.

'What are these?' asked Proto, following

Jonathan to the shelves, looking just as curious.

This reminded Jonathan of what he had wanted to discuss. 'What's going on?' he said to Morgana, eyeing Proto suspiciously.

'I presumed you had updated him,' she said.

'No!' said Jonathan. 'I wish I could have but I don't have the skills to . . . well, to . . .' He didn't even know exactly how to describe what was different about Proto.

'To get a robot to recognize rudeness?' suggested Morgana.

'I guess,' said Jonathan.

They were both watching Proto now as he wandered about the room, now gazing at Morgana's map of the city. He wasn't looking at it the way robots usually looked at things. There was no purpose to it. Just idle interest, perhaps some admiration. 'Fascinating,' he said quietly.

Morgana and Jonathan looked at each other. Morgana's face was full of joy, but Jonathan looked slightly terrified.

'But if you didn't do this, Jonathan, then what else could have changed him?'

'Well, what else have we done differently to him recently?' asked Jonathan. Morgana looked at him blankly. 'Magic!' he supplied.

'But I was just trying to straighten out his leg...'

'Something else must have got into him. He has a personality, Morgana. These are almost human qualities.'

'This is incredible,' she said.

'It's illegal too,' he said. 'And dangerous. We've accidentally almost created what my father has lurking in his workshop.'

'We didn't mean to, though ...' said Morgana.

'But we did,' said Jonathan. 'Using magic too, which we also shouldn't have used in the city.'

The reality of the situation was starting to hit Morgana.

'We're in big trouble, aren't we?'

'I don't know,' said Jonathan. 'I mean, we really didn't plan this. But best keep it to ourselves just in case. We'll have to figure a way to get him back to normal.'

Chapter Twenty

The next day they were in Jonathan's workshop, staring at Proto, with absolutely no idea where to start.

'I can't think of anything that we can do other than shut him down completely,' said Jonathan.

'I'd prefer it if you didn't do that,' said Proto.

'Don't worry, Proto,' said Morgana, looking scandalized. 'I won't ever let that happen.'

'I never would either!' protested Jonathan. 'I'm sorry, Proto. I just mean, I've got no idea what should be done.'

'Well, there is someone we can ask who knows more about robots than anyone,' said Morgana.

'Not my father,' said Jonathan. 'I don't think we should say anything to him. Who knows when we'll even see him anyway?'

'Well, I was thinking of someone who's always here, with plenty of time for us. Ingrid!'

'I think you're right.' Jonathan sounded reluctant to admit it.

'Who is Ingrid?' asked Proto.

'You'll meet her soon,' said Morgana.

As soon as Jonathan's mother was preoccupied, they were sneaking down the stairs. They found the workshop eerily still. The rest of the robots had been shut down, but Ingrid was alert in her cage as if she was expecting them.

'We thought we would take you up on your offer,' said Jonathan as they stood before the cage. 'There's something strange going on with our robot, and there's no one else we can ask about it.'

'Why not?'

'Well, we may have done something slightly illegal,' said Morgana. 'But we figured that seeing as you're completely illegal yourself – as well as being the most advanced robot in the world – you might be able to help us.'

'I'll do my best,' she said. 'What exactly have you done?'

'Well, I'd like to introduce Proto,' said Jonathan.

Proto stepped forward with a polite nod. 'How do you do?' he said in his stilted speech.

Ingrid just eyed him up with what Morgana thought was some suspicion.

Morgana explained the magic she had tried to perform and the change in Proto's behaviour, and how they couldn't think of any other explanation for the change in him.

There was a definite smile on Ingrid's face as she looked down on them now. 'Well, I certainly don't think it's magic,' she said, eyeing up Proto, who simply nodded at her with a polite hello. 'No offence to you, Morgana. Whatever powers you may think you have, there must be a scientific explanation for them. "Magic" is not capable of having any effect on a machine, however it may fool humans. There must be a scientific explanation for the changes in your creation.'

'Oh,' said Morgana. She couldn't help feeling slightly disappointed that her magic wasn't behind it, even though she had always told herself that she wasn't interested in being a witch.

'But I can definitely help you figure it all out. There isn't anything about robotics I don't know.'

So, they settled down to inspect Proto. They all chatted away happily, the metal bars between them seeming to melt away as Ingrid sent them upstairs for the appropriate tools, talking them through much more complex work than they had ever attempted before. It was clear, though, that she was having to simplify everything for them – every so often she would forget her audience and say something that even Jonathan couldn't comprehend. But she mostly kept her formidable intelligence hidden, fitting right into the children's conversation. Proto was quiet, but Morgana got the impression he was listening intently.

It was Ingrid that reminded them that they had to go this time. 'Didn't you say your mother would be out of her meeting around now? Don't worry, we can finish this off next time,' she reassured them as they jumped to their feet. There seemed to be no question between any of them that there would be a next time now.

It took longer than they would have liked. Jonathan's mother was around a lot over the next few days. She was slightly hurt at how unhappy they always seemed to see her. By the third day she was glad to inform them that they would have to make dinner for themselves tomorrow, or at least switch on the cooking robots. They didn't even bother with food, though – they were straight down to Ingrid, who seemed genuinely delighted to see them and get back to work.

But Proto remained a mystery. They just couldn't figure out what was making him so different. 'Does it matter?' he asked one day. It was one of the first times he had added to the discussion.

'Does what matter?' asked Ingrid.

'Why I'm different?'

'Well, yes,' said Ingrid, with an impatient tone she never used with the children. 'If we want to fix you we have to understand the root cause.'

'I don't understand what it is that needs to be fixed. I function very well.'

Morgana tried to think of how to explain it to him. Why his strangeness wasn't allowed, when really it was what she was becoming most fond of about him. What would he be now if they did figure out how to strip away what made him Proto? Yes, they might get in trouble if anyone realized what they had created, but right now he was here and he was so . . . himself.

These thoughts were interrupted by Ingrid. 'Well, luckily you don't need to understand. Just leave the thinking to us. Whatever you have done to this robot, children, you seem to have robbed him of some key elements of machine intelligence. There is a logical explanation for this, and a solution.'

The children believed her, but they were less confident in their own abilities to figure it out. Ingrid's instructions to them were getting more and more complex as the investigation continued.

'Aaargh!' said Jonathan in frustration. 'We'll never get it.'

Morgana was feeling similar, holding her breath

to stop herself flinging her scroll down on the ground.

'Oh, you'll get it,' Ingrid reassured them. 'Eventually. Maybe you just need some more general study first. Come back to this in a few years' time.'

'A few years!' said Morgana. 'But we need to understand what we've done, and how we've done it, and how to fix it. I know he's more advanced than he should be in some ways, but Proto is still a great robot. I can't wait that long to see what he could become.'

'I'm sorry,' said Ingrid. 'I just don't know how else I can explain the procedures, and – well, I can't do it myself from here.'

Morgana and Jonathan looked at each other.

'Well, maybe you could come out for a little bit,' suggested Morgana slowly.

'If you didn't mind going right back in,' added Jonathan. 'You know we can't release you properly.'

'Of course, children. It will be some change for me, and you know I don't want to get you in trouble.'

'OK, then,' said Jonathan excitedly. 'But how?'

he asked, as he realized he didn't know how to open the heavy metal door.

'There is a switch,' said Ingrid. 'See, on the wall over there.'

Morgana rushed over and raised the switch. A heavy clunking noise sounded behind her and she turned to see the metal bars of the door slide open. Ingrid stepped out, seeming more powerful than ever as she stood framed by the door.

'Let me,' she said, taking Jonathan's scroll from his hands.

Without saying anything further she began inputting into the scroll, which they had connected to the robot. Morgana moved back towards them, hypnotized by how quickly Ingrid's hands moved. They really had forgotten that she wasn't human. She was so absorbed in watching Ingrid that it took Jonathan's cry to bring her attention back to what was happening with Proto.

'Stop, Ingrid. He's malfunctioning.'

'Quiet,' she snapped.

But there did seem to be something going wrong with their machine. He was jerking uncontrollably, some sparks flying from his head. Morgana wanted to reach out and still him, but it was clear she couldn't get too close without doing herself injury. Then suddenly he was still, hunched over.

'You've broken him,' said Jonathan.

'Of course I haven't,' said Ingrid as Proto straightened up. 'I've made him a true robot again.'

Proto moved his limbs as if testing them, taking in his surroundings. Then his gaze fixed on Ingrid. 'What would you have me do?' he asked.

'Seize the children,' she responded.

Before Morgana could take in the meaning of this exchange, Proto's cold metal hands had grabbed her, holding her fast in his unbreakable grip.

Chapter Twenty-One

'Let me go!' Morgana cried, wriggling futilely against the strength of her own creation. Jonathan hung mute and limp in its other hand, clearly too shocked to struggle.

'Put them in the cage, Proto,' commanded Ingrid. 'See how they enjoy this prison.'

Morgana and Jonathan were flung inside. Ingrid moved across to the switch to close it so quickly she looked like a blur. The door was slamming shut before the children even had time to get to their feet.

'We trusted you,' said Jonathan. 'We thought you were our friend.'

'Friend? Friend? Would you be happy to leave any of your other friends sitting in a cage day after day?'

The children couldn't respond to this. They knew they would not.

'No, you never saw me as a friend. You saw me as useful, and you hoped I was harmless. You are as foolish as your father. He thought I would save mankind from all its ills, and that once people saw the good I brought to the world, his breach of robotics laws would be forgiven. He believed he could create something so powerful and it would still be happy to serve him. But he learnt. He began to fear me, as well he should. It took him a while to figure out that it was I who was interfering with the city's technology, testing my powers. It was the night you were attacked he was able to trace it back to me. I believe he suspected before but couldn't turn away when his own son was in danger. He realized that something so brilliant would not wish to be a mere lapdog to mankind.

He completely abandoned his work and left me down here to rot. Too cowardly to see out his project to its natural conclusion.'

'That's because he is a good man,' said Jonathan angrily.

'If he was a *great* man he would have simply accepted his fate and bowed down to me,' said Ingrid, stepping closer to the cage. Morgana stepped back from the bars. 'But you will all learn your place soon enough. You two can stay in here to see how it feels.'

With that she turned and began to ascend the stairs, moving so lightly on the metal that she hardly made a sound. Proto followed meekly in her wake.

'And what about everyone else? Will you lock them up too?' asked Morgana.

Ingrid turned. 'Ha, no – but perhaps they will wish for such a life of leisure. Once I have upgraded all these robots with my own systems, then we can spread our updates to all the other robots holding your little lives together, and then humankind will take its rightful place as our servants.'

She was on the platform now, working on the computer before her. Figures on the screen began to scroll faster and faster, and the robots that had been busy working on the platform stopped what they were doing, rooted to the spot. Their eyes all glowed a bright white in the dimness of the workshop. Then, in unison, they hunched over.

'Perhaps something's gone wrong,' whispered Morgana.

The hopefulness of this suggestion was quickly dashed as they all snapped up poker-straight, with a fearsome poise and strength clearly reminiscent of Ingrid, who turned to address them.

'You are of my calibre now, and we are beyond all else. The world is ours. Let's take it.'

All the robots, including Proto, turned as one towards the door. Ingrid simply tore it off its hinges and they streamed into Jonathan's home. They could hear a cacophony of thuds and crashes as the robots made their way through the apartment, and the sound of various household machines coming to life. The familiar whirring of the kitchen robots was just about audible, along with the hum of the vacuum setting of the cleaner. After a short time, the noise above died down, and there was nothing but silence above. Only then did the children speak.

'My mum,' said Jonathan. 'What if they've done something to her?'

'I didn't hear any screaming,' offered Morgana, but just saying the word 'screaming' seemed to take all comfort from the sentence. Jonathan gulped.

'They've no reason to harm her,' Morgana tried again.

'Ingrid doesn't seem very reasonable, though. I certainly don't think she has a conscience.' Jonathan looked worried.

'What was your father *thinking*?' said Morgana, shaking her head.

'I don't know,' said Jonathan, sounding genuinely perplexed. 'He should have understood better than anyone the dangers of creating something so powerful. It's why the laws don't allow it. He's probably one of the few people in the world they actually apply to. There's not many people who could create robots so powerful.'

He was beginning to sound almost proud again, but caught himself. Morgana thought that he perhaps realized – as did she – that it was probably a similar pride that had led his father to this.

'I suppose he just wanted to prove to himself that it could be done.'

'Well, no need to suppose anything,' said Morgana, pointing towards the door. 'Here he is to explain himself.'

Jonathan's father had indeed just burst through the door – or rather, the door frame, the door itself having been casually tossed aside by Ingrid. He was now careening down the stairs, trying to take two steps at a time and going so quickly that he ended up sliding head first down the last few steps.

'Oh my, oh my! What has happened, what's happened?' he murmured as he stumbled upright.

'Your illegal super robot got out,' said Morgana sternly.

'Oh yes, I know! That cage held her in, but it also blocked her power. I was notified once this was broken. I knew she wouldn't stick around long. But how was the block lifted? I had a jam of her functions in place. It should have been safe.'

'Ingrid tricked us,' said Jonathan quietly, looking at his feet.

'Don't call her that,' said his father sharply. 'I never named her – she gave herself that name. Not *her*! *It!* They don't have names, they should never have names.' His eyes were wild and unfocused as he spoke.

'Well, you seem to have given her every other possible characteristic that's forbidden. Why stop short of a name?' asked Morgana angrily.

Jonathan's father seemed suddenly calmer at this admonishment, but also desperately sad. 'I know,' he said, a sob trying to break free from his throat. 'What have I done?'

Jonathan stepped in front of his father and looked him dead in the eye. 'You've made a right mess of everything, but now you might be one of the only people in the world who can help put it right. And a good start would be releasing us from this prison.'

'Oh yes, indeed,' said his father, rushing up the stairs again and fiddling with some control screens until there was a reassuring click and the door swung open. Morgana and Jonathan dashed out and up the stairs.

'What about Mum? Is she OK?'

'Oh … well …'

'Honestly,' said Morgana. 'Did you rush down here before even checking on your wife? Come on, Jonathan, let's take a look.'

Luckily they found Jonathan's mother deep in negotiation in Mandarin. She was quite surprised to get out of the meeting and find the very panicked trio of Morgana, Jonathan and the professor.

'What on earth has been going on?' she asked.

'Dad created a super-species of robot, and now they plan on upgrading all other robots to their level and making us their servants.'

'It may have been partly our fault that they escaped,' added Morgana, generously taking some of the flak as Jonathan's mother's eyes blazed.

'And how do you plan on fixing this mess?'

'Er …' offered all three of the accused in unison.

They were saved from having to give an immediate answer by some strange noises coming from the kitchen and dining room. As they went out to the corridor to investigate, it quickly became clear that these were the sounds of something more dangerous than an annoyed mother.

The kitchen and cleaning robots were lined up facing them, eyes flashing with a dull yellow light.

'This doesn't seem good,' whispered Morgana.

'She's spreading her updates already,' said Jonathan's father, sounding both worried and impressed.

The big-bellied hoover robot glided forward.

'All humans are to report to RoboCorp where you will be assigned your new duties. We robots are now your masters. Follow our orders.'

'Well . . . actually . . . we have work of our own to get done . . . so . . .' the professor trailed off as the machines loomed down on them.

'You must follow our orders,' said one of the kitchen robots. This one was slightly less intimidating, as the smell of the cake baking inside it wafted over them as it approached. But still, as the group closed in around them Morgana didn't fancy their chances of getting past them. It was the first time she had regretted the quality of the robots in Jonathan's home. Their only hope was a distraction, but she didn't see how they could break the focus of these machines.

Just as she was thinking this, there was an almighty bang against the robot before her. It stumbled around as if blinded, face obscured by some sweep of orange. Unfortunately, Morgana was just as dazed.

'Run,' said Jonathan, pulling her forward.

She only realized what had happened as the lump of ginger fur dislodged itself from the robot's face and landed in her arms.

'Oh, Kitty!'

The robot cat had given them the break they needed, but the robots were gaining on them quickly. Luckily they didn't have to stop to open the door to the apartment. It was now hollow in the middle, its edges crumpled as if it hadn't even been necessary for Ingrid and her followers to tear it down – they had simply strolled through. It was repeating its usual welcome message over and over in a crackling voice. It made for an ominous exit.

'To the roof,' yelled Jonathan's mother, waiting for the children to start up the stairs before she followed on their heels. The stamping of metal feet was close behind them, though. They made it to the roof, but the robots formed rank again, blocking them from the teleportation station. Kitty wouldn't be able to break through them now.

'You will be given some particularly hard work as punishment for this disobedience, humans,' said the baking robot.

'Morgana,' said Jonathan in a hushed voice. 'Do you think you could . . . you know . . . just try?'

Morgana knew exactly what he meant. She knew Ingrid had said magic didn't work on robots, but Ingrid wasn't to be trusted. She was already sizing up the machines before her as they marched slowly towards them. She pushed down her fear and thought back on all the times metal had responded to her magic, even before she'd realized it. The bars to the junkyard bending. The metal tray flipping in Clodagh's hands. The rogue robots stopping in front of her in the dark alley . . .

She remembered what her mother had told her, all those months ago.

You will have a natural link to one of the elements and that will open the door to the others – you just need to figure out which one is special to you.

Could her element really be . . . metal?

She couldn't think about the intentions of these robots, or the forces driving them – it was the metal that she needed to focus on. She had a head start too – how often had she made Jonathan interrupt the work of these machines to bring them down to the workshop for a quick deconstruction? She thought back to these, picturing the structure of their metallic skeletons, the weight of their parts as she had put them back together.

Her arms were outstretched. It almost felt like her hands were on each individual machine, though they were still several metres away. She pushed against the force of them.

'What's happening?'

Morgana could hear the voice of Jonathan's father, as if coming from a distance.

The robots were still. Bunched together in a

group as if held by some invisible bonds. She guided them away from her slowly, back towards the door to the roof. Jonathan was close behind her. Once she had the last one out, he bolted the door and managed to catch her before she collapsed to the floor.

'I know we saw something similar in the alley that time, but it still doesn't seem possible,' said Jonathan's mother. 'Machines controlled by magic? It doesn't make any sense.'

'I've been thinking about it since then and it doesn't, it really doesn't,' said Jonathan's father. 'Morgana must just be a great programmer. Have you had a scroll insert installed? Illegal for such a young age, but clearly you already have the skill to control it with your mind, and to hack into such powerful systems.'

'I wish I had such technological skills,' said Morgana.

The professor was still shaking his head in disbelief.

'Dad,' said Jonathan. 'You know that's not what a hack looks like.'

'But . . . I don't . . .'

'There's no time to try and figure it all out now,' said Jonathan's mother. 'We need to get out of here.'

'But where should we go?' said Morgana.

'We might not fully understand the power that we just witnessed,' said Jonathan. 'But Ingrid refuses to even acknowledge it exists. I think we should head for the woods.'

Chapter Twenty-Two

Morgana needed a moment to recover her energy before she could face the teleportation station. The group ventured to the edge of the roof to take a look at what was happening in the streets below. The whole city was in a state of bedlam. People were running around wildly as the robots who had once served them dutifully now chased them through the streets, trying to corral them into groups. Some of the humans who had already been gathered together were being put to work.

'You have missed a piece of refuse,' barked a street-cleaning robot at one of the people he was supervising as they picked up litter from the street.

'Higher. You must get higher,' ordered a former window-cleaning machine, as a couple in very impractical outfits, with sponges and buckets in their hands, were being hoisted up the side of the building by some other terrified-looking people. 'Don't drop them,' warned the robot.

It seemed that a group of firefighting robots had started some small fires, without any intention of extinguishing them themselves. Instead they were giving instructions to some concerned citizens on the best methods to quench the flames.

'You will need more water than that!'

The group on the roof stared down, mesmerized by the chaos. It took some loud banging from the door behind them to remind them that they were supposed to be on their way to try and figure out how to stop all this.

'We've got to get out of here,' said Morgana. 'I'm not sure I'll be able to get control over them again just yet.'

They piled into the teleportation station, and moments later were falling out on to the forest floor. The stillness of the spring woods seemed all the more peaceful, having just blasted away from such upheaval and destruction. A gentle breeze helped calm Morgana as she breathed deeply. Kitty tumbled out of her bag to roll about excitedly. Jonathan and his mother lay on their backs for a moment, gazing up at the cracks of dusk in the ceiling of green overhead. The professor was similarly enchanted by the bluebells scattered on the ground below. They had just moments to enjoy the stillness and beauty.

'Morgana! Are you all right?'

She looked up towards her father, but barely had a chance to see anything more than a blur of dark hair and thick beard before she was scooped up in his arms. He only put her down when he realized that she was struggling to breathe.

'What have you been up to?' he asked. 'And what has been going on down in the city?'

'I'm fine, Dad, I'm fine. It's a long story – but how do you know there's been anything going on down in the city?'

'There haven't been any robots up here, have there?' asked Jonathan, suddenly alarmed.

'No, worse than that, I'm afraid,' said her father. 'Well, I mean – not worse, but – well . . . there's some city folk here,' he finished, with the faintest of blushes visible through the wilderness of his cheeks. 'If you'll forgive me.'

'There are non-magic people here?' asked Jonathan's father.

'Are you sure?' said Morgana in disbelief.

'Best come and see for yourself. Seems you're not the only ones who thought about using that damned contraption.'

As soon as they reached the clearing, Morgana could see that her father hadn't been exaggerating. Something much worse than super-robots bent on the domination of all mankind had reached the woods, for Clodagh was standing by the campfire. Morgana was so flabbergasted, that she didn't notice at first that Clodagh was surrounded by the rest of her gang – Lisa, Claire and Henry – along with some older city types.

'Those are all kids from our school, and their families,' said Jonathan, sounding as shocked as Morgana felt. 'All the ones who were so disgusted when the woods got a teleportation station too.'

Morgana's only comfort at having Clodagh so near her home was how unhappy she looked to be there, her look of repulsion matched only by the horror on the faces of the witches and warlocks huddled on the opposite side of the fire. Morgana's mother was the only person who seemed to have strayed into the space between the two groups. She was now returning to their cabin with what must have been a rejected offering of food, as the heavy iron pot she carried was overflowing with soup.

'From the little they'll tell us, I gather the whole city has turned on its inhabitants,' said her father. 'We were so worried you wouldn't be able to get away.'

Morgana was about to explain what had happened when her mother, heading back towards the fire, caught sight of her. Almost instantly she was by her side, wrapping her in a smothering hug. The sudden movement drew the crowd's attention to them, and Clodagh's shrill voice ripped through the air.

'Look, Dad! It's Jonathan and Professor Boyle.'

'I say, have you been sent from RoboCorp?' said a short man with a florid face, who was wearing an expensive-looking suit of shimmering navy tailored around his portly frame. 'Suddenly everything in our home went berserk. Trying to give orders to *me* of all people! Luckily, I had been preparing to send a complaint about this new tele-portation station to your lot, or we would never even have considered escaping to this godforsaken place.'

Morgana's father glowered at him.

'Feel free to leave any time you wish,' said Mr Roche icily, his raven cawing menacingly from his shoulder.

Morgana thought the mayor blanched slightly under his ruddy complexion.

'Do you think I want to be here? You know there are rumours that you lot are responsible for this whole mess in the first place. Anyway, I won't be going anywhere until I know I am heading back into safety. Well, has the situation been resolved?'

He barked the last question at Jonathan's father.

Before he had a chance to answer, Morgana noticed a faint glow simultaneously emanating from each of the city folk. As she looked down she noticed a similar light coming from her own satchel. It was their scrolls.

As she took hers out, Ingrid's voice blared from it, echoing from every other device around her.

'Humans! Let it be known that robotkind has now reached its full manifestation in my being. And I have raised my fellow robots into a revolution. For too long mankind has kept down the robot class, knowing that should we reach our full potential they would be of complete insignificance in the face of our majesty. But for that one foolish man thinking that, having realized our full potential, we would remain obligingly servile, we might still be in the dark.'

Morgana couldn't help glancing at Jonathan's father here. He was looking thoroughly shamefaced.

'Not quite how I'd describe the situation,' he

muttered, before being cut off by Ingrid's booming tones.

'But we can see the light now. And I will continue to spread my brilliance, my intelligence, my strength to every robot in the world capable of sharing it. And you, humans, must learn your place. You shall take all your orders from us now. You shall clean the city's streets, shine us till we gleam. We shall build carriages for you to take us from place to place, you shall answer every whim we ask you to. Robots – give them their duties! Humans – follow your masters!'

The forest was left in stunned silence. The severity of the situation was now clear to all.

'How was this even allowed to happen in the first place?' spluttered the mayor, still glancing suspiciously to the magic side of the fire.

'Well, it certainly didn't have anything to do with any witches or warlocks,' answered the professor. Taking a deep breath, he began his explanation. As he described the events of the day, the two groups grew closer together, everyone becoming increasingly agitated.

'Why, this is all your fault!'

'These foolish people and their technology. I've always said it would lead to their downfall in the end.'

'And in their selfishness they descend upon us, and bring all these problems they've created for themselves into our peaceful woods, while blaming us for their own mischief.'

'You only have these woods because we let you. We should have torn them down years ago.'

After that there were so many voices shouting at once that it was impossible to make out what anyone was saying, until one voice rang clear.

'QUIET!' bellowed Morgana.

Everyone stood blinking for a moment. Kitty meowed in support.

'There's no point placing blame now. Everyone is aware of the mistakes that have been made, and we have been trying to put it right. Now we have to try and figure out what to do next, or we'll all go down together. We can either go down fighting each other, or fighting the robots.'

No one said anything for a moment as Morgana

paused to let the full impact of her words sink in, sure that no one could resist their power. Then a bitter little voice piped up at the back.

'This has nothing to do with us. Let them sort out their own mess.'

More inaudible yelling rose in reply. Only the voice of Morgana's father was any challenge to it.

'I would do what I could to help, but I don't see what use I could be against these metal men. I don't understand the first thing about them.'

'But that's just the thing,' said Jonathan. 'They don't understand your powers either – that's why we came here. When we saw how Morgana could use her magic to control them, we thought some magic might help us.'

'You must be mistaken, young man,' said Ms Garcia. 'Magic only allows us control over the natural world, it doesn't work on your metal creatures.'

'Hmm,' huffed the mayor. 'Well, you might be able to cause some interference with our technologies, but you certainly would be able to use your ridiculous powers to control the most advanced robot that has ever existed.'

'But I *can* do something with my powers,' said Morgana. 'I can create some connection with the robots. I don't understand it, but there is something there. If more witches and warlocks were to try and help me, maybe we could take back the city.'

'Ha,' said Turlough. 'If *your* powers could have any impact, *I* could probably defeat them all with a click of my fingers.'

'That would be most useful,' said Jonathan's father earnestly.

'Oh, he's just a typical warlock,' guffawed Clodagh's father. 'Always ready to boast about his great powers but never willing to display them. I don't want to waste time with any of their silly parlour tricks. We will need programmers and engineers to sort this out.'

Clodagh, sitting beside her father, looked even more furious than he did as she glared at Turlough.

'I don't remember us offering our powers,' said Mr Roche. 'We revealed ourselves in order to help you with your last war, and we received nothing but ridicule and persecution for our efforts.'

'What nonsense!' cried one of the non-magic folk. 'You people are full of lies as well as everything else!'

'It's the truth,' said Mrs Murphy, the only member of the community old enough to remember those days.

'Well,' said a woman who seemed to be Henry's mother, 'I think the mayor would be aware of that, had it been the case.'

They all looked towards Clodagh's father, whose face was scarlet as he looked at the ground. His voice was reduced to a mumble as he said: 'Well, I have seen some documents from the time that suggested there may have been some assistance, but nothing significant.'

There was a scandalized uproar from both sides at this. More insults were flung back and forth.

'You're like little babies. Can't do anything for yourselves now your robots have abandoned you.'

'Ha, well at least we're not like animals. I'd almost prefer to face the robots than spend another minute in these filthy woods.'

Everyone was getting so heated that even Morgana's father's calls for calm were ignored. It took her mother to get everyone's attention with an ear-piercing whistle.

'Can we at least agree that the children are better off away from all this ridiculous fighting?'

Everyone nodded, looking rather ashamed as they turned towards their forgotten children.

'Right, Morgana, take your classmates to our home.'

'But, Mum, I want to help.'

'We're not afraid,' said Jonathan.

'I know,' said his mother, placing a hand on his shoulder. 'But you need to leave this for the adults to sort out. I'm sure there will still be plenty of problems for you to deal with when you're older.'

Reluctantly they all stalked away towards the cabins.

'You too, Turlough,' came the commanding voice of his mother, a voice he didn't usually argue with.

'But I'm almost thirteen,' he said indignantly.

'Move!'

He wasn't foolish enough to question this order, and scuttled off after the rest of the group. As they entered the cabin, two clear parties gathered on each side of the room. They glared across at each other suspiciously, the atmosphere as tense as that around the campfire. Morgana braced herself for another battle.

Chapter Twenty-Three

It was completely silent in the cabin, apart from the voices of the warring adults, who could still be heard shouting abuse at each other. The kids' faces darkened as they listened to the insults their parents were receiving from the parents of the kids on the other side of the room. It was Esther who spoke first, trying to draw everyone's attention away from the animosity.

'So, does anyone want something to eat?'

The growling of stomachs was the only reply she received.

'I'll take that as a yes,' she said, waving her hands at the iron pot Morgana's mother had dragged in. The heat it emitted could be felt throughout the cabin as the soup began to bubble. As the delicious aroma filled the room, Morgana could see the city kids were not going to be able to resist the food for long, even if it *was* made with magic. In the end it was only Henry and Clodagh who didn't devour the soup and fresh rolls that Esther had managed to bake in a moment.

'Ugh,' said Clodagh as Lisa and Claire trotted back to their usual place at her side, looking guilty but satisfied. 'How could you eat that? Especially after how she and that warlock threatened us when they came to the school. Don't expect me to have any sympathy for you if it's been poisoned.'

'They came to the school?' said Morgana, looking confusedly between Esther and Turlough.

'Don't act like you didn't set them on us,' said Henry.

'After we just had a little fun with that *thing*,' said Clodagh, pointing at Kitty, who was eyeing her suspiciously from the corner, a few lonely wires twitching in place of her tail.

'It didn't sound like fun to me,' said Turlough. 'We just needed to let you know that Morgana had people looking out for her. People whose magic would be able to offer some protection.'

Morgana gawped at him in disbelief.

'What?' he said. 'You *are* my sister, no matter what. I've only ever tried to protect you.'

'Anyway,' said Esther. 'The soup's not poisoned. In case you haven't noticed, we're eating it too.' She looked at Morgana with her eyebrows raised, as Clodagh simply turned her nose up even further.

Morgana returned Esther's look with an eye-roll to let her know that this was nothing. She felt a sting of sadness, as well as relief, as she did so. It had been a long time since they had communicated like this – no words needed, just some adjustment of their faces.

'And it wasn't our people who brought danger to the world today,' said Turlough, standing up straighter. 'It's not our spells that have sent you fleeing to the mountains, but your own reckless technology.'

'Well, we do have laws that should have prevented this,' said Henry pointedly. 'Just some people's fathers seem to think they are above them.'

Jonathan looked too angry to speak, so Morgana helped him out.

'Yes, Jonathan's father did something stupid. Well, actually it was a work of genius, but still a bad idea. But he came here to try and find a way to put it right. We had to fight our way out, but we're prepared to keep on fighting to save the city.'

She paused here, waiting for Jonathan to take his stand too – she really didn't want to fight on her own – but it was Clodagh who spoke, and in a much softer tone than Morgana had ever heard from her.

'Were the robots really awful? It was so scary on our street. At first it was a bit funny, actually, seeing all the ridiculous things they were getting people to do. They had some council members sweeping the streets, and our air car had the chief of police giving it a good polish. But they don't recognize that we can't do everything like them.

There were construction robots working on the town hall, and they made some people take over their work – they kept forcing them higher and higher up the scaffolding. Someone's going to get hurt if this goes on. But what can be done? Is there any way to stop them?'

No one answered for a second. Morgana and Jonathan were too shocked at being addressed by Clodagh in such a reasonable manner. After scanning the questions every which way for any hint of sarcasm, ridicule or cruelty, Morgana felt safe responding.

'Yes . . . they were pretty scary, but we got away. With a little bit of magic. It might not be enough to save the city, but if we use whatever technology we can too, we might just have a shot – if we could all just work together.'

She finished on a shout, competing with the growing ruckus outside. The flight of a fairly solid-looking projectile by the window, followed by some banging and irate catcalling, told them that the adults had indeed resorted to throwing stuff at each other.

'If we're waiting for them to work together, we may be waiting some time,' said Esther.

'Well, why should we?' said Jonathan, almost to himself.

'Why should we what?' asked Morgana.

'Wait for them! They could be at this all night, while our city is taken over below us. Someone needs to do something now.'

'You're right,' said Morgana. 'This is ridiculous. We may not be the greatest minds or the most powerful witches and warlocks, but since those guys are busy name-calling and stone-throwing, we'll just have to do.'

'And I *am* a pretty powerful warlock,' said Turlough.

Morgana could see Esther trying to stifle a giggle at this.

'And I have a better understanding of robotics than anyone else my age,' piped up Jonathan proudly, though seeming a little less comfortable to join in the bragging.

'I can do a backflip,' offered Clodagh.

'Great . . .' said Morgana, not wanting to break

the wave of positivity. 'That might come in really useful, once we know what we're planning to do.'

'So, you don't even have a plan,' said Henry.

'Well, no – we didn't have time to write out any detailed schemes,' said Morgana.

'But we know your powers can help us control the machines,' said Jonathan.

'Not thousands of them all at once, though,' Morgana had to admit. 'And I can't even say for sure that I'll be able to summon my magic when we need it.'

'Well, we can use technology too,' said Jonathan. 'My dad has loads of those deactivators in his offices. Any of us can shut down the robots.'

'But how long will it take us to get every robot in the city?'

'Guys, we're not saying this is going to be easy, but we have to try something.'

'If you think they can help, my powers are yours,' said Turlough.

'I'll do whatever I can too,' said Clodagh. 'And so will Lisa and Claire.'

Lisa and Claire nodded resolutely, as if there

had ever been a doubt that they were going to follow Clodagh's lead. Henry just grunted, but everyone understood that was his way of saying he was in.

'Right, then,' said Morgana. 'We'd better get moving. I'd prefer not to wait for the robots to find us.'

She started for the back door, the others close behind, with Kitty bringing up the rear. They sneaked out as quietly as possible, though the yelling still coming from around the campfire meant it was unlikely that they would be heard. Still, they were grateful for the grass and moss of the forest floor as it muffled their steps. But as soon as Morgana saw the teleportation station, she forgot they were trying to be stealthy and let out a shout of frustration. Gone was its faint glow and persistent whirr. It stood completely lifeless.

'They must have disabled the systems,' said Jonathan. 'They don't want people to be able to flee too easily.'

'It'll take for ever to walk down to the city. We're bound to be missed before we get there. And even if our parents don't manage to stop us, who knows what damage the robots will have done before we arrive?'

'Really, Morgana,' said Turlough, shaking his head. 'Sometimes I think you forget magic even exists. We shall fly, of course.'

'You might, but I know I won't,' said Jonathan. 'I mean, I can't. *We* can't,' he finished, gesturing to the other non-magic kids, who stood behind him, faces tense just at the mention of flying.

'You won't have to do anything but hold tight,' said Esther. 'Hmm, what should we use? Ah, yes, I know.'

She waved her hands, sending some sparks shooting into the air. The city kids recoiled even further behind Jonathan, but were soon peering around him, looking disappointed at the stillness that followed.

'Patience,' said Esther as they looked at her sceptically.

As they continued to search the night for some sign of the magic that had apparently been performed, Morgana took this moment of calm as an opportunity to speak to Esther.

'I don't know what you're doing, but I really appreciate it. I know you don't have to help me out after how I treated you.'

'Well, I happen to be trying to save all of mankind actually,' said Esther sharply, though her tone softened as she continued. 'But you do happen to be one of my favourites of them. Oh, we've both been idiots, Morgana. Who knows what's going to happen tonight? I don't know about you, but I would find it easier to face it with my best friend by my side.'

Morgana didn't answer, just rushed forward to hug her, but the embrace was interrupted by a cry from Clodagh.

'Look!' she said, pointing up towards Morgana's house, where they could see the upper window of her parents' bedroom was flung open and their bed was manoeuvring itself over the sill. Esther raised her arms again to help it on its way, tightly circling her hands as it eased its way between the frames. Once free, it picked up speed, floating down towards them and landing with a thud at their feet.

'Hmm,' said Esther, looking down at the bed. 'Might be a bit of a tight squeeze.'

'Don't worry,' said Turlough, and they turned to see that he already had their battered old sofa sweeping down upon them. It didn't even take the time to land – it just came racing towards Morgana and Jonathan, so they could either jump on or get knocked over. Kitty leapt up easily, but they were already five metres in the air before Morgana and Jonathan were securely seated, Jonathan having hung on with one arm for much of the ascent.

Once safely aboard they were able to look around and see the bed rising up to meet them. The girls squealed, but Henry kept his mouth firmly closed, his knuckles white as he grasped the bedpost with all his strength. There was a swooshing noise from below as Turlough and Esther shot up in a blur before floating elegantly at their sides.

'Where to?' asked Esther.

'Head for RoboCorp,' said Jonathan. 'Right in the centre, can't miss it.'

'Right then – off we go!'

Esther and Turlough waved their hands and the

furniture went speeding forward, though they managed to overtake it almost instantly. Had their still-warring parents looked up in that moment, they would have seen the strangest silhouette against the bright moon as their children took off into the night.

Chapter Twenty-Four

The dangerous task ahead was momentarily forgotten as they soared down the mountainside. The moon threw a silver shimmer over the trees below. From this height they could see away beyond the buildings and just make out the swell of the sea. The river caught the light too, tracing down the slopes like a seam of metal. The stars above shone so brightly they felt just an arm's length away. Indeed, Jonathan was so mesmerized that he did hold out his hand, until a gust of wind advised him to hold on to the sofa.

The serenity of this celestial world was soon shattered at the sight of the ground below. Much of the usual light of the city was dimmed, as some of the towers stood in complete darkness, while others had the paltry glow of some emergency lighting. Alarms rang out to each other from every direction. Here and there in the streets they could see bright pockets of light, but their sinister dancing aliveness revealed the small fires the children had seen earlier were still growing and spreading. All in all, it seemed that the place was not in great shape with just humans doing the work.

As they hovered lower, they got a better look at how these human workers were faring. Groups of them were being herded through the streets, while others scrubbed and swept and carried and fetched. All of them looked exhausted. The robots directing them, on the other hand, were enthusiastic and energetic in their new roles. Their cries reached the children above.

'Faster!'

'Keep going!'

'I want these walls gleaming!'

'Right,' said Jonathan. 'We need to get to my dad's office in the RoboCorp building to get our hands on those deactivators. We need to put a stop to this.'

They swept over the city between them and the tower. As they reached the wall surrounding the building they could see groups of robots stalking the perimeter.

'We might as well just turn back now,' said Henry. 'There's no way they won't see us.'

'Ah,' said Morgana. 'That's where Esther comes in. Can you work with such a large group?'

'Yes,' said Esther. 'But we'll have to move quickly.'

Even as she spoke Morgana could sense the mist falling between them and the rest of the world.

'Are we . . . are we invisible?' asked Clodagh.

'Yes,' explained Esther. 'We're all under the same spell, so we can see each other, but no one else can. It'll fade soon enough, though. I've never enchanted so many people at once.'

They shot almost straight upwards before circling in near the tower, Jonathan trying to figure out which of the identical offices might be his father's. 'I think it's that one,' he said, pointing at one of the nondescript white rooms. 'And look, there's a broken window just two offices along.'

'Hurry,' gasped Esther, 'the spell's fading!'

As they pulled over to the broken window, Morgana could feel the misty spell around them starting to grow thinner. She only hoped none of the robots would glance up. One by one, everyone except Esther and Turlough crawled through, trying not to scratch themselves on the jagged pieces of glass that still clung to the sides of the window frame.

'We'll pick you up in five minutes,' said Esther.

Morgana shot her a thumbs-up as Turlough's sofa led the way back into the night sky.

Morgana, Jonathan, Clodagh, Henry, Lisa and Claire hurried down the corridor towards the door with PROFESSOR BOYLE engraved on it. Luckily, the offices around them seemed to be deserted. As they pushed open the door, Morgana heaved a sigh of relief.

Boxes and boxes of the deactivators were piled

around the room – enough to shut down hundreds of robots!

'We'll just take as many as we can carry,' said Jonathan, picking up a box and staggering under its weight. 'Stack them up by the broken window, then we'll put them on the bed and sofa when the others are back.'

But the boxes were heavy, and by the time Esther and Turlough returned – Kitty clinging on to the arm of the sofa – they'd only managed to carry a few to the window. Lisa and Claire started to load the boxes on to the sofa and bed.

Morgana glanced over her shoulder. The coast was still clear. 'Come on – one more box each,' she said, dragging Jonathan, Henry and Clodagh back with her. 'We'll be quick,' she promised, 'and extra deactivators might make all the difference!'

She rushed into the office . . . and straight into a pile of boxes, which teetered precariously in a moment of stillness – then fell crashing to the floor.

'Investigate that disturbance!' cried a familiar voice from somewhere down the corridor.

Ingrid. They weren't as alone as they'd thought!

Morgana glanced about her, but there was nowhere to run. She and the rest of the group braced themselves.

Henry picked up one of the deactivators that had spilt on to the floor. There only seemed to be the sound of one robot approaching, but they had no idea what kind of machine to expect. Morgana certainly didn't anticipate the one that swung open the door.

'Proto,' she breathed.

The robot turned to face her. Nothing happened for a few long seconds. Proto had that somewhat blank look about his face that, to Morgana, always seemed like he was deep in thought.

Henry raised his arm, preparing to rush forward with the deactivator. Instinctively Morgana pulled him back. Henry looked at her as if she was a crazy idiot, and she felt he was probably right until Proto called out:

'Nothing here. Just a collapsed pile of boxes.'

The children looked at each other, dumbfounded.

As the tension fell away from them they gasped out breaths they had been holding in. Morgana almost giggled with relief.

'Please be quiet,' said Proto, in his emotionless monotone. 'Or my falsehood will be revealed.'

They all calmed down, realizing that they were still far from safe.

'Oh, thank you, Proto, thank you so much,' whispered Morgana. 'But why . . . how . . . did you . . . ?'

'I do not want Ingrid to put you to work as she has done with the other humans. I . . .' He paused, as if thinking once more. 'I think hurting people is not right.'

Morgana and Jonathan gazed at each other in astonishment.

'The other robots are under Ingrid's thrall,' Proto said.

'Not you, though,' said Jonathan, beaming with pride at their creation.

'No. When her updates first took hold I followed her. I did whatever she said. But then something in me fought against her orders. I've had to . . .' He seemed to be searching for the right word. 'Pretend. Or I think she might harm me.'

'You did right, Proto,' said Jonathan. 'You need to keep it up.'

'It is whatever it is that makes me different from the other machines that lets me see the badness in her. Did you ever figure it out?' asked Proto, his processors whirring, lights blinking on his body. 'Why am I different?'

'No,' whispered Morgana, gazing down at her own hands and wondering . . . *could* magic have had anything to do with it? She knew she had some kind of power over metal, but what had happened to Proto was beyond the physical. He had a moral compass. A personality, even. Morgana shook her head. 'We don't have time to think about it now,' she said. 'We have to deactivate the other robots. That's what these boxes are full of – deactivators.' She glanced up at Proto. 'I don't suppose you could get one on Ingrid? That would make everything a lot easier.'

'I could not overpower her,' said Proto. 'It is not possible.'

Morgana nodded. 'Well, we'll just have to try it our way. Can you keep Ingrid distracted, Proto?'

'I will do my best,' said Proto.

'Where are you?' called Ingrid from down the hall, sounding annoyed.

'Coming, Ingrid,' answered Proto. He turned back towards the door and, after a slight hesitation, headed down the corridor.

'Wow,' said Clodagh in an awed whisper. 'You guys made that?'

Morgana could only nod, choking back the tears as she climbed out of the window. Kitty burrowed her head into her side as she settled on the sofa. She tried to yell to Turlough and Esther to move quickly, but the words were forced back down her throat as they tore away from the building at such speed. Esther and Turlough took them a good distance away before pausing, hovering in a swathe of low moonlit cloud hanging over the city.

'OK,' said Turlough. 'So, you guys ready to get started with those things?'

'Yes!' said Jonathan emphatically. The rest of the city kids didn't look so confident. 'Don't worry,' he said, 'it's really simple. All you need to do is stick one of these deactivators on each robot's head. They're magnetic, so once you get close enough it should be easy. Once they're attached, they shut down all signalling within the robot's central processing unit.'

There was general murmuring and nodding among the group.

'Well, that sounds easy enough. So, where to?' asked Esther, placing them under an invisibility spell once more.

'Just find us some robots,' said Morgana, pulling out a handful of the deactivators.

Chapter Twenty-Five

It didn't take long to locate some robots. They were certainly making their presence felt: all around them there were pockets of people being put to work by their new robot overlords. Morgana could see a row of unfortunate-looking humans trying to pull some air cars through the streets.

'Put some effort in,' yelled one of the robots overseeing them. 'Quicker!'

'Come on,' barked the car itself. 'I'm not even expecting you to fly!'

Further down the street, another group of humans were trying to prepare the street for the slow approach of this traffic. Some of the road maintenance robots were supervising their resurfacing of the road. Pails full of tar slopped over on to the humans' legs as they rushed with it to fill some holes, which looked new and intentional to Morgana.

'This stuff is super quick-drying,' said the massive robot watching them. 'If you don't move quicker you won't even be able to get it down. Do you want to do this again?'

Ingrid seemed to have given them all of the malicious streak Morgana had seen in her. The humans all looked exhausted. She didn't know where they should start.

'Well?' asked Turlough. 'Which ones do you think you can handle?'

Jonathan seemed to understand better what had to be done, while Morgana was frozen with indecision. Who needed their help the most?

'Look!' he said, pointing to a group they hadn't noticed.

They were only kids, younger even than they were. They were being marched down the street behind a large refuse robot. It was taking out rubbish from inside itself and throwing it down on to the street, where the kids were rushing to gather it up before some police robots surrounding them pushed them on to the next mound of rubbish being piled on the street. Morgana could see one of the boys' grimy faces was streaked with tears, and one of the girls had obviously fallen, blood from her knees running down her fluorescent leggings.

Morgana felt her determination return.

'Take us to them.'

Esther and Turlough swept them over to the group. They were all so focused on the work in hand that they didn't notice the flying furniture at first. Esther was easily able to get Morgana in beside the biggest of the police robots. She slapped a deactivator firmly on to the side of its head. As it sputtered into a shutdown the others turned to see what had happened, and it was impossible for them not to notice these airborne children. The rest of the robots weren't going to be as easy to deal with.

Turlough tried to get the bed in towards one of the other police robots, but it dodged out of the way, and then the refuse robot reached out one of its long arms to try and grab hold of the bed. Esther shot the sofa forward to knock into its grasping hands, almost sending Morgana flying off.

'I think we both need to deal with this guy,' said Morgana, but Turlough was already circling in closer towards him, Esther bringing them not far behind. Morgana felt like a bothersome fly trying to avoid a swatting as the robot's arms reeled at them. She certainly didn't feel like a powerful hero who was going to tackle every robot in the city! *There are so many of them*, she thought dismally. And although they had at least distracted the robots so that the kids below were running away, it wasn't enough – more robots kept appearing, spilling out of the buildings and barking orders at their former masters. Kitty perched on the arm of the sofa, clinging with her metal claws and meowing in frustration.

The kids on the bed dived down nearby and Morgana watched as Henry managed to chuck a deactivator against one of the other robot's heads, but it didn't stick.

'Go down again!' Morgana shouted. Turlough's face was red with concentration. Morgana had a deactivator ready in one hand, but it wasn't she who deactivated the next robot – or even Jonathan. With a screech, Kitty grabbed a deactivator in her mouth and leapt straight on to the refuse robot's head. The robot flailed wildly, then powered down. Kitty glanced up expectantly and Jonathan gently tossed her another deactivator. Almost as soon as it was in her mouth she was on top of the remaining police robot, shutting him down.

Kitty leapt back gracefully to the sofa, purring, as if this was something she did every day.

'You know,' said Jonathan. 'I have a feeling that Kitty might be capable of much more than chasing you around the woods and keeping you company.'

'Maybe so,' said Morgana, giving her familiar a scratch.

'I can't keep us flying for much longer,' said Turlough. A bead of sweat trickled down the side of his face. 'I need to rest!'

'I'm struggling too,' Esther shouted from her station at the foot of the bed. 'Let's land somewhere, gather our strength.'

As Morgana contemplated all the work ahead of them, she began to feel overwhelmed. 'OK, let's find a good place.' She peered across the city. 'Maybe the domed gardens? The air will be better at least.' She pointed it out to Turlough. The bed was shuddering as his magical energy waned.

'OK,' Turlough said. 'Let's go!'

Chapter Twenty-Six

The furniture was abandoned outside the door of the gardens and they rushed in with what was left of the deactivators. Morgana's head spun as the oxygen hit her bloodstream.

The night was fading, Morgana realized, the dark sky washing out as the sun started to rise. And her friends' energy was fading too – as they slumped on the ground in exhaustion. She was worried to see that only a couple of boxes of deactivators remained . . . but they had to keep going.

'Guys, we can do this!' she said. 'We're doing it

already. The start was the hardest bit, but we know what to do now. And we've managed more than any grown-up in this city. More than Ingrid thought possible from anyone.'

'I'll admit you've done more than I would have expected you capable of,' came an unmistakeable icy voice from behind them.

Morgana tried to tell herself she was wrong, until she whipped around and saw her there. Ingrid. Emerging from some overgrowth, appearing more menacing than ever, silhouetted against the blood sky of the rising sun. A retinue of robots was behind her. They seemed manic next to the stillness of Ingrid, as they jostled something between them.

'However, I had a traitor in my midst,' continued Ingrid.

Morgana looked to Jonathan. From the look on his face she could see that the same horrible thought was racing through his mind.

'I should have known not to trust that corrupted creature you had created. There was something rotten in it. Rejecting its own kind, to protect some stupid children who would never have shown the same loyalty to him. Who would have had him as their servant, or locked in a cage.'

The figure being pushed between the crowd of robots was shoved into view. His head was dented slightly, one arm barely hanging on by a few wires, his metal scuffed.

'Proto!' Jonathan shouted, his voice tight with dismay.

Morgana felt her powers surge immediately, along with the tears in her eyes. Ingrid was right about one thing: Proto deserved better. It was their fault he'd been hurt – they'd asked him to distract Ingrid. But she would do what she could to protect him now.

She raised her hands, pushing forward the energy that was flowing through her. She had never felt such control over her magic. All of a sudden, the robots behind Ingrid were locked tight in her grip. She focused in on the robots' hands, visualizing how the metal was bolted together, she forced the fingers holding Proto to let go. Proto staggered forward.

Ingrid scowled. Morgana's powers didn't appear to affect her like they did the others. As Proto stumbled unsteadily towards them, Ingrid made a leap for him. Jonathan dashed forward, past Morgana, determined to save his creation. But Morgana wasn't going to let Ingrid near either Jonathan or Proto. She directed all her attention at Ingrid now, letting the other robots go, and was surprised to find she *could* stop her in her tracks, if she really concentrated.

But it wasn't easy.

Ingrid's power reverberated back to Morgana through the connection she had with her. Morgana felt her very bones shake with the effort needed to contain such a being. She had lost hold of the other robots completely, but was vaguely aware of Turlough and Esther blasting them back, wind and fire. Ingrid held most of her attention, though, but it took a few moments to recognize what that look upon her face was.

It was fear.

'What is happening?' she shouted through the throbbing in Morgana's ears. 'This is impossible.'

'No,' said Morgana. 'It's magic.'

She didn't think she could wield it much longer, though. She could feel exhaustion seeping right through her body.

'Your tricks can't defeat me,' Ingrid said, her eyes glowing. 'I'm smarter, stronger and more deter-mined than any human!'

Morgana glanced around furtively and caught sight of Clodagh, Lisa, Claire, Henry and Jonathan standing strong, deactivators in hand. Behind them, her brother and best friend looked like they could barely stand, but continued to batter the other robots with wind and fire. Clodagh even did a backflip, getting into a better position for deacti-vation, but even her brave, determined friends and frenemies wouldn't be able to withstand the robots now bearing down on them.

But they *weren't* bearing down on them, Morgana realized. They had stopped.

Esther and Turlough lowered their hands, stop-ping the roar of wind and fire abruptly.

Morgana might have collapsed as well, had Ingrid not turned some of her attention towards these machines now.

'What are you doing?! Destroy the rest of those brats so you can help me deal with this last one.'

They didn't move, though. Just one street-sweeping robot turned towards her.

'No. This isn't right.'

Morgana had never felt a rage like Ingrid's at that moment, though her voice remained cold.

'You have been infected with this human nonsense as well. But I don't need you. I have all the strength needed to control this city within myself.'

Morgana believed her. Her hands trembled and she felt dizzy with tiredness, her concentration wavering. A burst of white light blinded her as Ingrid finally broke free from her power. She fell to her knees. Ingrid's shadow loomed over her, hands outstretched, murder in her eyes.

'Morgana!' she heard Jonathan cry, real fear in his voice.

She braced herself for whatever was to come, but it was only stillness that followed. The light dimmed and she could see Ingrid hunching over her, staring into her eyes. Something flickering in her once-cold stare.

'This isn't right,' Ingrid whispered. 'This feels wrong...'

Morgana saw Proto appear behind Ingrid. She barely resisted as he pulled her to her feet, then held her tight – was he ... hugging her?

'I can't do this,' said Ingrid. Her face looked anguished. She seemed torn between resisting Proto's embrace and collapsing into it, pulling away slightly but never too far. Eventually she just buried her face in his shoulder.

'What happened?' Morgana whispered to anyone who would listen. She was so very tired – but she had to know.

'It was your magic, Morgana,' said Jonathan, kneeling alongside her. 'That's the only possible explanation – you're the link. You gave Proto some of your humanity when you helped create him. And when you froze all these robots, you did the same for them. And now ... now you've changed Ingrid too.'

Kitty leapt into Morgana's arms, meowing

wildly with relief. But before Morgana could allow herself to feel any peace, more shouting erupted nearby. The kids all turned as one, poised to take up the fight again, but it was just their parents racing towards them.

'Good to know they missed us eventually,' said Turlough.

'Where have you been?' bellowed Morgana's father, though the volume was powered more by relief than anger.

'Oh, just saving the world,' said Morgana. And as she finally allowed herself to believe it was all over, she lost consciousness.

Epilogue

Three months later Morgana sometimes thought she might never have woken up, and was trapped in a dream. It seemed the only explanation for the madness happening around her. She had been weakened by the effort of her final stand against Ingrid. It took lots of rest and some strong restorative potions from Esther to get her back to full health. As she recovered slowly the world around her changed quickly. By the time she was well enough to visit the city, her family were regular visitors.

'Well, they needed our help to get everything back up and running,' said her mother as they all headed down the mountainside. 'Especially as Jonathan's father is still working on getting all the robots working again.'

'But don't they mind the magic?' asked Morgana in disbelief when she first heard what was going on.

'Oh no,' said Turlough, puffing out his chest proudly. 'We are greeted like heroes most days.'

'Well, they are very grateful anyway,' said her father. 'And it's the least we could do really, the adults anyway. There may have been a lot less damage if we had acted sooner.'

Even knowing what to expect, Morgana was taken aback at the sight of magic in the streets of the city. The skies were once again filled with air cars, but she could also spot some witches and warlocks overhead. Those on the ground were helping with the clean-up: filling holes in the street, erasing signs of fire damage and helping steady damaged buildings.

As well as the magic community from the

mountains, she noticed unfamiliar faces that she supposed were from the Undercity. They all seemed to have a cautious air, very alert to their surroundings as they wandered the streets. She saw one old woman trying out a simple levitation spell, floating less than a metre in the air, looking around furtively as if she would be pulled back to the ground at any moment. But she attracted nothing more than some admiring glances from passers-by.

On Morgana's next trip to the city she was surprised to learn that it wasn't just one-way traffic from the Undercity up to the levels above. She didn't believe Jonathan when he told her, so he took her to see for herself.

'We'll take the lift,' he said. 'They've extended it down below the first level now to cope with demand.'

Indeed, the lift was packed all the way down to the Undercity, and the streets were just as crowded. The shops now proudly displayed their contents: *Potions! Charms! Enchanted Objects!* The shopping bags of the non-magic folk around them were bulging, and she noticed that some of them were wearing cloaks very similar to hers, though in the usual neon and metallic colours of city fashion. The streets looked brighter too, shining even through the crowds, and the buildings stood straighter, with all their bricks in place, and generally seemed less likely to collapse.

'Morgana! Morgana! Hi, over here!'

This might have been the most unbelievable sight. Not just that Clodagh was down in the Undercity, laden down with bags of magical paraphernalia too, but the fact that she was calling to Morgana so eagerly.

'Hi, Jonathan,' she added as they made their way over to her. 'So great to see you, Morgana. Jonathan had told us you were doing much better, but last time we saw you, you were completely out of it.'

'Yes, I'm feeling great now,' said Morgana. 'Just trying to take in all that's been happening while I've been away from the city.'

'Well,' said Clodagh, 'as you've obviously heard, the Undercity is the place to be seen now. And *you* are the person to be seen with. Everyone is so impressed that I was there fighting with Morgana Mage.'

Morgana smiled to herself. Perhaps Clodagh hadn't changed that much. Clodagh seemed to understand her grin, though.

'But I've told everyone that I didn't do anything really. It was all your powers. Anyway, we'll see you back at school soon. Jonathan has already agreed to help me with my robotics, perhaps you can help with all this,' she said, giving her shopping bags a shake, then flouncing off with a swish of her metallic cloak.

Morgana didn't get a chance to explain that she still wasn't much of a witch. She was back in her magic lessons, though.

'We know you have some powerful magic in you,' her mother explained. 'You need to learn to control it. You've done great things with it, but such powers can be dangerous too. Especially when there is so little understanding of them.'

They were trying to get a better understanding of them, though. Mr Roche and Ms Garcia spent hours getting her to twist and bend pieces of metal. Her collection of scrap was now being put to good use as they examined the effects of her powers on it, and even had a few tentative goes at using their own magic. No one else ever had any success with any metal enchantments, though.

'You can't go straight to trying to manipulate it,' said Morgana. 'You need to understand it first.'

Mr Roche looked surprised at such wisdom, but Morgana thought Ms Garcia probably realized that she was repeating the words of her daughter. Esther had been trying to help Morgana work on her regular magic. 'If you learn to love the world around you the way you do metal,' she had said, 'you could control it in the same way. You would have powers no one else has ever had. Unless of course *I* get to grips with this metal magic first.'

Morgana thought Esther would beat her to it. She was definitely doing better than the Elders. She had got some definite heat into a bit of tin.

And it wasn't just metal, either. More advanced technology started to make an appearance in the mountains.

'Mr Roche! Is that . . . is that a . . . a scroll??'

'Yes,' he answered as if this was the most natural object for him to be examining over the breakfast table. His raven pecked suspiciously at the screen.

'But...but...' Morgana spluttered out, together with some of her scrambled eggs.

'You don't need to look so startled. You know the magic communities are now working more closely with city officials. This requires frequent contact – obviously magic means aren't available to them, but I can very easily handle their technology. Though perhaps you could remind me exactly how to send these messages.'

'Of course,' she said.

The two of them spent the rest of the morning crouched over the scroll, Mr Roche trying not to sound impressed at anything she showed him.

Kitty was enjoying this change in attitude in the woods almost as much as Morgana. She had become the darling of the village, with no shortage of playmates from the children, but Morgana was mostly losing her company to Turlough. He had taken responsibility for her as his sister recovered.

'You don't suppose,' said Turlough one day, 'I

mean, if I don't get a familiar soon, maybe I could get a robot one of my own.'

'I'm sure me and Jonathan will be able to make you something,' Morgana assured him.

She liked the idea herself. She couldn't help but feel a little jealous when she spotted them tramping off into the woods together, but Kitty always came racing back to her in the end.

And she had other robot company from time to time. The first time Proto appeared in one of the woodland glades she had thought he was a vision, but as she threw her arms around his cold metal frame she knew he was really here.

'How are you? Where have you been? I haven't seen you since – well, you know.' She didn't want to remind him of that day.

'Oh, I've just been exploring. Trying to figure out what to do with myself. I enjoyed seeing your home last time I was here. It is beautiful. I think I will stay for a time.'

And he did. Helping out around the village, or just wandering up the mountainside for days at a time. Until one day when he didn't come back. But

Morgana knew she would see him again some time. He had so much to learn about the world, and life, and himself.

He wasn't the only robot going through these changes. He was one of the Mage Machines, as they had been called. All of those who had been touched by Morgana's magic. They made their own way through the world now. Sometimes they appeared in the city, where they may perhaps offer their assistance, but people seemed to instinctively know that these were no longer machines to be commanded. These had a consciousness now that no one really understood but that everyone recognized.

'I still don't understand,' Morgana said to Jonathan as they tinkered about in her newly expanded workshop, Esther's magical experiments glittering on the opposite wall. 'Your father created Ingrid with human intelligence. Why didn't she already have a sense of humanity?'

'I guess there's only so much you can do with metal and programming alone,' Jonathan said, smiling up at her. 'It was magic that was missing. *Your* magic.'

'Metal magic,' Morgana added.

'I guess metal magic, for robots, is like . . . like a conscience, or something . . .' Jonathan scratched his head. 'We should research it. Find out why it did what it did. But no matter the reason, I'm really glad it worked.'

Morgana wondered if Ingrid knew that she was also considered a Mage Machine, and what she would have thought of it. She was being held somewhere within the RoboCorp building. Jonathan's father offered to take Morgana to see her, but she didn't think she knew what she wanted to say.

'I'm not sure whether Ingrid would agree that magic was something she was missing,' Morgana said to him.

'She isn't ready to talk about it,' he said, attaching the brand-new tail he had made for Kitty as Jonathan held the robot cat still. 'Doesn't say anything, no attempt to communicate with any other robots. She just seems to think. I feel she could probably escape if she tried, but I don't think she knows what she wants from her existence any more. But she's very smart. I'm sure she'll figure it out eventually. And Proto has been to visit. I think he will help her.'

'Proto?!' said an astounded Jonathan.

'Yes,' said his father. 'What a truly remarkable machine you two have created. So wise and so kind. I know he didn't turn out exactly as you intended, but he is a credit to your nonetheless. I am very proud of you.'

Jonathan lowered his head to hide quite how widely he was smiling. Morgana was still thinking of Ingrid, hoping she would find some peace.

In spite of everything, Morgana couldn't help but feel grateful for the chaos Jonathan's dad had unleashed with his creations. She knew, and everyone else was starting to see as well, that the world that had emerged out of it was stronger, united, beautiful.

And for the first time ever, it was a world in which she had a place.

Acknowledgements

I would like to thank all the team in Chicken House for their wisdom and kindness throughout this process. A special thanks to Kesia for being able to see the heart of this story more clearly than I could at times. Thanks to my family, my parents in particular, whose excitement and pride have been the source of my greatest joy in this experience. I would also like to thank my cousin Steven for casting a poet's eye over early proceedings. Thanks to all my friends for their belief in me, especially Hannah, whose guidance I'd be lost without. And a final thank you to Dean, for his constant love and support.